# Growing Wings

This book is a work of fiction. Names, characters, businesses, organizations, places, events, and incidents either are the product of the author's imagination or are used fictitiously. Any resemblance to actual persons, living or dead, events, or locales is entirely coincidental.



ISBN: 1-4825-6794-6
ISBN-13: 9781482567946
Library of Congress Control Number: 2013903525
CreateSpace Independent Publishing Platform,
North Charleston, SC

# Growing Wings

K A Neemeyer

2013

# Dedication

I want to give a sincere thank you to Nancy, Judy, Tracy, Raynelda, and Kayley for taking your time, during the writing process, to help me out. I also want to give a big thank you to Pam. I appreciate your honesty and how you are never afraid to give me your opinion, if I want it or not. That means a lot to me. But the greatest thank you would have to be given to my husband. You have always been there to tell me that I can do anything I put my mind to and to push myself to succeed. I would have never started nor finished this book without you cheering me on. You are my biggest supporter and I am eternally grateful to have you by my side through it all.

# chapter I

As Jenna sat on the beach, with soft sand as a pillow below her sun-touched skin, the July heat surrounded her like a warm blanket. A cool breeze left goose bumps on her arms which were quickly taken away with the warmth of the summer sun.

Every few moments waves from the ocean hit the beach and sounded like an unfamiliar dialect to her ears. The waves seemed to try and speak to her with every crash against the sand, but were carried back out before she could understand. As she watched them move, they looked as if they were trying to reach out and beckon her to them.

Jenna shielded her eyes as the sun reflected off the waves and appeared as if it were dancing on the water, while the colors created a breathtaking silhouette against the miles of ocean below. The descending sun frolicked on the water and gave her the feeling that it wanted her to dance along. The sound of the waves, the sand moving beneath them, the bubbles and foam popping on the beach, and the sun dancing on the ocean left her in a trance. She lost track of time.

Suddenly, a firecracker ruptured the air. She was pushed out of her trance and the sweet laughter that followed brought her back to her surroundings. As she watched children run past her, she saw that the sun had almost disappeared and it had turned into nightfall without her even noticing.

With the darkening sky above them, Jenna watched the silhouette of children as they ran with shimmering sparklers in their hands. They tried to write their names in the night air before the light faded into the darkness.

Watching them made her smile, and when she saw the grins behind the crackle of lights, it lifted her spirits even more.

Jenna heard moms calling to their young ones to be careful and watched others as their arms embraced the one they loved. As she looked at them, she had a feeling of happiness and sadness in the same moment. So she reached down and caressed the soft hair of her young dog, as he rested his head on her lap.

She was surprised that despite all the movement and noise that surrounded them, he was calm and relaxed. Although, she liked the soft rhythmic breathing against her skin. It helped her to not feel alone, even among all these people.

A loud boom made them both jump and the show began. The darkness was penetrated with explosions of sound followed by bright patterns that lit up the night sky. Shapes seemed to be momentarily etched into the darkness before being replaced by another. Flowers bloomed before her eyes and faded just as quickly. Sparkles of color radiated and drew beautiful canvases of art. Streams of twinkling lights cascaded down and dove into the ocean below as if they were being swallowed.

Jenna was mesmerized by the amazing show of colors, soft glow from bonfires, and wafting aroma of burning pine. She memorized all of the tastes of salt being lifted from the ocean, combined with the smells and sounds so they could not be lost. And during each explosion of light, Jenna noticed the shadows and movements of the people surrounding them. They looked like they had been in slow motion with the light display above.

When the final display of fireworks burst in the night sky, the cheer of the crowd was just as loud. The people, who had seemed to be shadows hidden in the remaining smoke, came back to life as more wood was put on the campfires to continue the night's festivities. And just as fast as the display was over, the remarks of wonder and how much time it had taken to put on the display took its place. The explosions of light quickly faded and were replaced with s'mores being made and children getting sleepy. And as Jenna looked out to the water, she saw that the ocean's waves even seemed to relax and lose energy after the firework display had finished.

So, with the last sparkler extinguished, she decided to take her memory and make her way home. She gathered up all her belongings and headed to her car. As she walked, she could see periodic bursts of color light up the dark sky from left over fireworks being ignited. And as she drove, the car momentarily lit up with a brief brightness that was reflected in her dog's brown eyes as he stared out the window.

Parking in front of her house, after the short drive from the beach, Jenna was happy to be home. She felt drained and her eyes weary from the day's events. As she opened the front door to her house, she was immediately at ease.

The aroma of vanilla candles and a faded smell of garlic from dinner still lingered in the air, while the air conditioner hummed through the vents and the ceiling fan whirled slowly up above.

As she walked through the door she turned on the light and exposed the colors of the walls and décor. A theme with seashells and starfish, which she had collected through the years, expressed her love of the ocean and her fascination with its creatures and animals. She displayed a large portion of the shells under the glass of her coffee table next to a big overstuffed couch and love seat, both in soft beige. And to keep with the theme, she had soft carpet installed, for added coziness, and had painted the walls soft blues and greens with white trim to go throughout the house.

She threw her belongings on the carpet beside the couch. Then she followed Shadow to the kitchen and watched him devour his bowl of food as if he hadn't eaten in days. When he was done, he lapped up some water and droplets fell from his mouth as he walked back towards the living room. He rubbed his mouth on the carpet, to clean his face, and then disappeared quickly down the hall.

Jenna smiled as she shook her head and watched Shadow go towards the bedroom. Then she grabbed a cold beer from the fridge and opened it. Taking a long drink, she enjoyed the coldness on her throat before heading towards the bathroom. There, she started the shower, got undressed, grabbed her bottle of beer to bring with her, and stepped into the water that was spraying down from the shower head. She let the water pulsate against her skin until she felt like all of the sticky sand from the beach was off of her. When she finally felt clean she let the heat relax her and enjoyed the contrast of the cold beer against the hot steam surrounding her.

After swallowing the last of her drink, Jenna stepped out of the shower and wiped the steamed mirror with her towel and gazed at the green eyes that looked back at her. Her skin looked smooth and clear and she admired the good tone she had for being in her early thirties. She was happy with what she saw, when she looked at herself, and was proud she did not fall to the peer pressure of the media of what a woman should put on her face. She had always thought she shouldn't have to conceal who she really was and felt blessed with what people called "natural beauty". Even though, she had to admit that she would never call herself beautiful, although she would catch men glancing towards her from time to time.

Stepping away from the mirror Jenna dried off, got on the scale, and threw her hands in the air, happy with her achievement. She had always felt a bit chubby throughout high school and college and was proud of what she did for herself and wished she had done it years ago. It had taken months of exercise and sweat to get to where she was, and she was very happy with the end result. And now that she lived by the beach in Maryland, it was good to feel secure in a bathing suit.

After drying off, Jenna walked to her bedroom to get dressed but first shook off her towel so she could inspect her naked body in a full length mirror. As she looked at herself, she turned to inspect her back and saw her tattoo and remembered how scared she was when she got it.

It had been only a couple weeks since she had moved to Maryland that she got the courage to visit a local tattoo shop. Nervous if she was making the right decision, she fumbled through countless books to find the perfect design. As she looked through the pages, she remembered reading that black butterflies could symbolize a new, strong but subtle life after undergoing a period of transformation. It also was said that they could symbolize a rebirth and a new beginning. This would happen after the caterpillar had encased itself for a while in its chrysalis, and then emerged more beautiful and did not dwell on what it used to be. It began a new life.

Jenna had overcome a traumatic time in her life and she felt she was going through a change herself. She wanted to have a new beginning. She wanted to become a strong and beautiful woman.

So after much thought of what to choose she selected a butterfly, but not just any butterfly. She selected a Pipevine Swallowtail for the tattoo that would mark her forever. It was a beautiful specimen that was black with bluish green hind wings and was flawless.

A bald man, covered with tattoos from the top of his head to down as far as she could see, positioned the needle on her lower back. It felt like a knife on her sensitive skin and she had to squeeze the handles of the chair to keep from running away screaming. But after he was done she looked in the mirror and admired the swollen skin with beautiful artwork on it.

Twisting her waist to get a better view, she saw the tattoo had a dark chrysalis hanging from a thin branch with only one leaf. The new, transformed butterfly rested on the newly opened chrysalis with its wings wide open. The Pipevine Swallowtail looked majestic and gave Jenna a symbol and new hope for her future. She remembered it had taken days for the swelling to subside, and even now, five years later, she thought it was worth the pain.

Stepping away from the mirror, Jenna threw on an oversized t-shirt and walked through her house checking to make sure all the windows were secure. Every night was the same ritual. She had to make sure the whole house was locked up to get a good night sleep.

After assuring herself the house was safe, she went back to her bedroom and sat down on the edge of her bed with her feet dangling. Her long brown hair fought against her as she tried to comb through it. She cursed the wind from when she had been at the beach for tangling it. Trying not to think about the snarls of hair, she thought about the wonderful day and evening she experienced before her thoughts went to the next day's work. She beamed just thinking about it.

Jenna had always enjoyed her job as a freelance photographer. It gave her a lot of flexibility but still was a challenge and she loved both. However, as she yawned, she knew that adventure would be tomorrow and right now she was exhausted. She needed to get ready for another busy day so she set the comb on the nightstand, slid under the covers, and closed her eyes.

# chapter 2

BLINKING HER EYES against the morning sun light, Jenna awakened to soft whimpering and wet kisses on her hand. She rolled over in her cozy bed, with the overstuffed comforter, and was met with big brown eyes and a wagging tail.

Shadow, her sweet little snowball of a dog had always known how to get her out of her bed with his wiggling and whining. He was a Bichon Frise, which was a smaller dog breed that was very social with straight white hair and a tail with long hair that curled towards his back. He had big brown eyes, a black nose and lips, and what looked like the perfect black eyeliner around his eyes.

"All right, all right, I'm getting up," Jenna moaned. She pulled herself up and Shadow started to whimper with excitement when he saw her feet touch the floor. He jumped off the bed and followed her down the hall, his eyes watching every move like he was making sure she was going in the right direction.

As they entered the kitchen Jenna grinned and shook her head. She liked that every morning involved the same routine.

Shadow would dance around in front of her as she would grab a treat from the cabinet. She would hold it in the air and he would stand on his two back feet and twirl on circles and then sit on his two back legs, like a ground squirrel, to get what he wanted. Finally, he would run to the back door to go outside.

Slowly sipping her hot coffee, Jenna watched Shadow as he rolled in the grass outside and thought of the first day she had held him close to her. It had been shortly after she moved to Maryland that she heard about some puppies being rescued from a puppy mill and she couldn't get to the animal shelter fast enough. Then, when she saw Shadow for the first time, he looked like a big cotton ball with legs, and he licked her face until she had started laughing. He was her best friend from that moment, and still was. Now, after five years, he had become her alarm clock, traveling companion, and her closest friend. Shadow had made everything easier to endure and she felt blessed to have him in her life.

Closing her eyes and taking in a deep breath, Jenna smelled an ocean breeze come through the kitchen window she had opened. The smell reminded her of what was to come. This was her ideal kind of day. She was going to be able to hang out by the water and take pictures of the annual sandcastle competition. It was close to home and she loved to be by the water. Perfect.

As she swallowed the last of her coffee and went to get dressed, Shadow was underfoot the entire time. Jenna jumped over him to get to her closet, and picked out some lighter fabrics to wear and French braided her hair so she would not have to fight against it again tonight. Before she doused her skin with suntan lotion, she grabbed her favorite sunglasses and slid them to the top of her head. She grabbed a beach bag filled with bottled water, snacks, and camera, then preceded to the beach.

After a short drive, she arrived at the shore with Shadow and her jaw almost dropped as her feet touched the sand. The place where, just hours ago, they had witnessed a display of spellbinding colors had been replaced with a completely different sight. She had to try and remember if this was where they had been the night before. And still, she could not believe the difference.

The bonfires had been cleaned up and replaced by buckets and shovels. Sparklers were now broadcasting microphones along with cameras to record the growing popularity of the sand art. The smell of burning wood was replaced by the sweet scents of sun tan lotions, wafting on the ocean breeze, and the number of people was twice as many as the night before.

She looked around and developed a feel for her surroundings and got ready to go to work. Jenna rolled her shoulders, grabbed her camera from her bag, and watched as the competition got ready to start. Knowing it would begin with the children and move up to teens and finally the adults she knew the talent would also grow with age. Capturing it all was the biggest challenge.

The competition began and Jenna snapped pictures of the children as they worked on their designs. During the process, their small bodies seemed to have as much sand on them as the castle did. The children would get their hands filthy with the sand then ran to the ocean to clean them, and came back to put them right back into the sand again. Jenna couldn't help but laugh.

After the children were done, judges walked around and handed out ribbons. The children's joy seemed angelic as they showed their prize to their parents and friends. Jenna made sure to catch the sparkle in their eyes to print on paper later.

She walked around and captured every smile, grin and tear from all the children she could and then began to photograph the joys and sorrows of the teens and adults. Their expressions varied from wonder that their sand creation had worked, to pure joy that it had not collapsed. And, of course, some were angry from creations falling from the weight of the sand. Others were frustrated, kicking sand in the air, feeling they had wasted their day. Jenna would snap their pictures before they stormed away.

As she walked around and took pictures of their work, she couldn't help but be astonished how the competitors could create such magical designs. Jenna thought it was breathtaking every year she saw it.

The elegant archways and castles with drawbridges had such detail. Along with the carved patterns in the mermaid tails and lion manes seemed to come to life. Trains, teddy bears, fairy tale creatures and so much more were created with mere sand.

Jenna chuckled to herself and loved the idea of being involved with something so creative. She liked the notion that these people could construct their creations with sand and she produced hers with a camera. She liked how she could capture the ideal smile or glance that would be missed otherwise. She liked taking an event and making moments of it frozen in time forever, caught with the lens of her camera.

For the most part, she was able to read people's emotions and she felt that gave her an advantage. She tried to be there in that moment to snare the image. She loved being at the perfect place, at the perfect time, and taking pictures brought that challenge alive.

But after a couple hours of taking pictures, the sun began to bear down and the day got hot quickly. Right after the competition ended, Jenna was ready for a break and walked down the boardwalk with Shadow by her side. They headed to Jenna's favorite ma and pa diner.

She quickened her pace, wanting relief from the sun burning down on her. She knew that the diner would give her that relief and more. Shadow seemed to know just where they were headed and he started to tug on the leash to get there faster.

As they arrived at the diner, Jenna sat down, with a plop, at her favorite table that offered a perfect view of the beach while it still got plenty of shade in the afternoon heat. She wiped her forehead with the back of her hand and shook her legs to relax the muscles. Within seconds, Kathy, one of the owners, brought out a glass of lemonade for Jenna and a bowl of water, with ice cubes, for Shadow.

Kathy was in her sixties but she acted like she was still in her early forties. She always wore shorts or capris, all year round, and had on a different t-shirt every time Jenna saw her. She was a bit overweight, but it never seemed to bring her spirits down, and she always wore bright red lipstick with half of it gone from her biting her lips throughout the day.

Over the years Jenna watched as wrinkles got deeper in Kathy's forehead and whatever streaks of blonde hair she had left turned silver. She had become a mother figure to Jenna, and Jenna respected her that way too.

"Good afternoon, Miss Kathy. How is the day going?" Jenna asked as she looked at Kathy, but then looked down just as fast. She stirred her lemonade and watched the ice cubes dance within the glass.

Kathy looked at Jenna over her eyeglasses, which changed to sunglasses with the sunlight as they spoke. Her silver hair was tied back in a tight bun and her t-shirt and shorts were covered with flour. She turned in a circle to show the flour, covering her from head to toe. "Well, Jenna, let me tell you a little about my afternoon. John was making biscuits just now, and I guess I was in the way. I was minding my own business and he grabbed a handful of flour and threw it right at me. And then he grabbed another handful and threw it as I was trying to run away. The nerve of that man. Sometimes I don't understand what goes through his mind." She had a stern look on her face and spoke with displeasure.

It was difficult for Jenna to hold back a smile with Kathy being so serious with flour everywhere; including her eyeglasses. Jenna kept her head down and watched Shadow try to catch an ice cube from his water, like a child trying to bob for an apple.

Kathy glanced over at Jenna and saw the hidden smile on her face and started to smile herself. She took her hand, wiped it over her t-shirt then smeared it across Jenna's cheek, leaving a flour trail and laughed.

"Now don't make me part of the fight." Jenna giggled and thought back on all the things she had witnessed through the years of knowing Kathy. There had been eggs in Kathy's hair, hands stained with green dye and her favorite was Kathy's scorched eyebrows. They had laughed about it for days until her eyebrows grew back.

Kathy and her husband John were a couple Jenna admired. She wanted a fun relationship like theirs for the rest of her life. Jenna had met them, here at the diner, shortly after she had moved to Maryland and felt blessed to find them. They had taken her under their wing and became her good friends and parent figures. The diner was their home away from home and Jenna noticed, through the years, they were here more than their own house. Of course, they talked on the phone periodically and Jenna had been to their house a few times for dinner, but if she needed them, this is where they usually were until seven or eight at night.

Kathy plopped in the chair next to Jenna's. "Whew! It has been a long day already."

Jenna watched as Kathy sat down and thought she looked uncomfortable. The sides of the chair were squeezing her plump hips, but she didn't give any impression of it bothering her as she tried to wipe the flour from her clothes. The flour would float with the soft breeze and when the breeze changed directions, the flour was right back where it started on her shirt. She gave up trying to remove it and reached down and rubbed Shadow's soft hair. Shadow wiggled with excitement. He jumped in her lap and cleaned some of the flour from her arm with his tongue. He squirmed and licked her and tried to get to her face to clean it too.

Kathy pulled on Shadow's collar softly to prevent him from licking her anymore. "Oh, my little one, you're sure happy today, although I can't think of a day when you weren't. What a wonderful dog you are." Kathy said as she ruffed up Shadow's hair on his head.

Jenna watched Kathy and Shadow and laughed to herself. She turned her head and looked out past the diner and appreciated that she was fairly content with her life. Quietly she whispered to herself, "Just forget the past and live in the present. No one's going to hurt me anymore. I won't let them."

Jenna and Kathy sat in silence at the table and watched people walk by in the scorching afternoon sun. After a few minutes, one of the tourists caught Jenna's eye as he walked towards them. He was tall and it seemed like he had not handled the hot weather very well. The summer heat was bearing down on him, his shirt was soaked with sweat, and his cheeks were as pink as Shadow's tongue. He tried to appear like he was okay but Jenna could tell he was miserable and felt sorry for him. She nudged Kathy, who then looked up and followed Jenna's line of direction and saw the man too.

Kathy set Shadow on the ground and pushed up from her chair. "Wow, haven't seen one like that in a while." She reached down and rubbed her legs that now had an impression from the chair pushed into them. She tilted her hand over her eyes, to shield them from the sun, and called out to the man. "Hey sir, would you like to try the best lemonade on the coast?"

The man glanced up at Kathy, said nothing, and continued to walk ignoring her request.

"Umm. Hey." Kathy fumbled for words. She motioned for him to sit down and had a sound of desperation in her voice when she spoke. "I'll throw in a fresh baked blueberry muffin for free. Haven't had any complaints yet."

The man's steps slowed and he turned towards Kathy. "I guess I could use a little break, thank you," he said in a deep voice. He walked over and sat at a table next to Jenna. He grabbed a few napkins from a silver dispenser on the table, wiped the sweat from his forehead, and let out a loud sigh.

Kathy hustled into the diner and as she stepped inside the door she glanced back at Jenna and mouthed *He's cute* before disappearing inside. Jenna rolled her eyes, looked away, and fumbled with her lemonade glass. She twirled the melting ice cubes within the pulp from the fresh squeezed lemons and took a long refreshing drink. Looking over the top of her glass, she glanced over towards the man who sat down at the table next to her and watched as he stared out at the ocean. She gazed at him while she took a drink from her glass, and liked what she saw.

He looked like he was in his early thirties, like her, and was quite handsome. She noticed his hair was the color of sand but, from where she was sitting, she couldn't see the color of his eyes. Looking down, it looked like he could be well over six foot tall from his long legs stretching out under the table. She gazed at his bare legs and could see that he took care of himself from the muscle tone showing on his calves. He was freshly shaven with a decent haircut and he looked like some sort of businessman. This made Jenna wonder if he was a visitor or if he had recently moved here. But there was something about him that she was attracted to and she couldn't put her finger on what it was.

Shadow started to prance under the table and then sat up like a ground squirrel to get the man's attention. He pulled on his leash to try and get closer and when that did not work he started to whimper and then finally barked.

Jenna tried to calm him down with no results. "Shadow, stop that. Not everyone comes here to see you," she said to Shadow to try and quiet him.

The man absently looked at Shadow and then at Jenna before he smiled. "Cute dog."

Jenna met the man's eyes and nodded before she looked back towards the beach. Her heart started to pound hard in her chest. She couldn't figure out what was wrong with her.

Immediately, without hesitation, her thoughts turned negative and she started to wonder if he would end up hurting her if she would talk to him and begin a relationship. She knew she had never met this man before, but she could not relax. Every time a man looked at her or tried to talk to her, she would automatically assume the worst from his intentions. She knew it was her past that was making her feel this way and wished she could make it stop.

But there was something different about this man's gaze that held hers for just a split second, and drew her in. His gaze scared her. No, it didn't scare her, it made her heart flutter!

# chapter 3

JENNA FOUND HERSELF back home after making an excuse of an appointment to get away from the diner.

"That was embarrassing," she said to herself.

She couldn't believe how situations like that seemed to find her. She tried to do a nice thing by getting Kathy to have a guy stop and cool down and it ended up being an uncomfortable predicament. And to make it worse, Kathy kept trying to get her to talk to the guy and all Jenna wanted to do was leave. She had felt warmer than usual, just by being close to him, and she felt like Kathy was trying to set her up for a date.

She knew Kathy was being harmless by trying to get them to converse, but she didn't feel comfortable with it at all. Kathy knew Jenna's past and Jenna was mad that Kathy didn't respect how she felt about dating or men in general. She was upset with Kathy and needed to forget the whole situation.

Jenna threw her bag on the floor and plopped onto the couch and let out a big sigh. She felt out of sorts and needed to clear her head. She snapped her fingers and knew just how to do it.

Walking to the kitchen, she grabbed herself a big glass and her favorite bottle of wine from the refrigerator, and headed out to the backyard. Once she examined the yard for anything or anyone that wasn't supposed to be there, she settled in her lounge chair, poured herself a glass of wine and took a big drink. Liking the taste of the wine on her tongue, she swished it around in her mouth to enjoy the flavor longer.

Shadow jumped on her lap and twisted and turned until he was comfortable and Jenna laid her head back on the chair to unwind from the day. She took another swallow of wine and looked up to see it was a gorgeous evening. The sun was setting and was leaving the most exquisite mixture of blues and pinks streaked across the sky. The clouds looked like big pieces of cotton candy that had been thrown into the air and left to float there. The breeze was soft and cool while the warmth from the day still lingered on her skin. She smelled the ocean in the distance and heard the seagulls flying to the cove, or their favorite resting place, for the night.

Jenna felt content where she was and took a deep breath. Enjoying her surroundings, she allowed her thoughts to float back to the scenario at the diner and thought of the man she had met there. She marveled that a simple gaze from him could have such a large impact on her emotions. She hadn't felt like that in years, if ever.

Jenna shook her head and tried to push the thought of the man away. She sipped her wine and closed her eyes. She envisioned that she could see waves crashing onto the soft sand of the beach. The man from the diner walked towards her slowly with a soft smile on his face.

Relishing in the moment, Jenna lingered a minute before her eyes snapped open with a mixture of fear and excitement. She pushed away from the daydream and took a drink while looking around her yard. She smiled at what she saw.

There were flowers growing from the summer sun and butterflies were dancing around them. The grass was a beautiful shade of green and freshly mowed. She saw the trees swaying with the breeze above the short fence surrounding her yard. There was no one there except for her and Shadow.

"Nope, no man walking around here," she whispered to herself.

She laughed at the thought of the man, or any man, entering her life and laid her head back again to try and unwind. As the clouds floated by, her thoughts got away from her and slowly drifted back to a time in her life that was not so good.

Through the years, Jenna tried to put the memories behind her but had not yet succeeded. The thoughts always seemed to seep back into her mind and were like watching a scary movie every time. And even now, as she tried to push them away, her thoughts began to float back on a dark cloud to that time in her life. It was a time when she was young, naive, and had fallen for Neil.

She had been in her twenties but she had always been shy and had never been involved in too many relationships before him. When she had first seen him from a distance, she thought he was unlike any man she had seen before. He had the "bad boy" image and she was instantly attracted to it and him. He was tall and lanky and said all the right things at the right times. His brown hair and soft blue eyes made her weak in the knees and she felt intoxicated when she was near him. She thought he was the greatest man on the earth from the first time he spoke to her and was proud to have him in her life. She wanted him for herself and always felt like she was going to have to fight for him.

But he had found her at a weak moment in her life and wooed her like no man had before, which made it easy for her to fall for him. He was always there to open doors and sent flowers with sweet promises attached to them. He bought her clothing which was not her quite her style, but she would wear it to make him happy. He would take her to dinner and was always so attentive when she talked about her family and friends. Most of all, he made her feel special and she drank it in like sweet nectar. Soon curtains were drawn over her eyes and she could not see the man he really was.

After a short few months, he had a way of making her think that everything he said was the truth. He would twist her words so when she knew she was right he could make her feel like she was wrong. And in the end, she always felt she needed to apologize to him for even trying to argue.

Eventually he found a way to distance her from her family and friends, without her even noticing what he was doing. He would make little comments to degrade her family or imply that they were not good enough for their perfect relationship. Then, when her family and friends would make remarks how Neil was beginning to control her, she began to question it herself.

She would tell Neil what they said and he would twist their words so Jenna would believe they were jealous and did not want them to be together. Neil would hug Jenna and said he would be heartbroken if she ever left him. He told her that he could not live without her and that he would go crazy if he ever thought she was with someone else.

Jenna's heart had ached when she thought about Neil being so distraught and did not want to upset him or cause him any pain. She loved him. Or, at least she thought she had.

Overtime she believed every word from his mouth and became confused with what was right or wrong with her own feelings. She felt that she had to believe Neil since he loved her and wouldn't hurt her. He had told her that all the time.

Slowly, she began to question everything her family or friends would say and began to believe that Neil was right and she needed them out of her life. It was like she had been brainwashed to act a certain way, dress a certain way, and live a certain way how he wanted her to. She lost sight of who she used to be.

This went on for over a year until they finally moved in together with the promise of marriage coming from his lips. Excited to be together, they moved into a small two-bedroom house that Neil had found. It had not been taken care of for years but he told her he was sure *she* could make it into a proper home.

It had wood floors throughout it and when Jenna looked outside, as she scrubbed years of dirt from them, she could see the nearest neighbor was at least a block away. Neil had told her that he liked the privacy so they could have their time together without anyone interrupting. Jenna agreed and would just smile and continue cleaning as she watched Neil leave to meet up with his friends.

Over the next months she tried to make a home of the small house but the money they made seemed to disappear in the bar with him and his friends and she didn't say a word. Then after a couple more months, late payments of the phone ended in it being disconnected and Neil convinced her they didn't need it anyways. He said it was just telemarketers and other people he didn't think she needed to talk to. This, of course, separated her completely from her family and any of the friends she had left. And through it all, she could not see that he had purposely isolated her from all that she loved and made her dependent on him and only him.

Then, that following spring, his car broke down and he took hers to drive and left her completely isolated. And of course, he never bothered to take his to the shop and she would have to ask permission to use her own car. If he didn't want to take her somewhere, then she didn't go. It didn't matter that the car had her name on the title or that she had paid for the car, she willingly gave it up to make him happy. That was her most important job, to keep him happy. She allowed it all to happen without knowing what he was doing.

After months of him coming home late with no excuse, and her having no transportation to go find him, she had enough. Finally, when he stumbled home from the bar at two in the morning, she got up the courage to tell him how she felt and that things needed to change. She wanted their relationship to work but she felt like she was falling down a hole and could not get out.

She started to ask him questions and made accusations about where he had been, the perfume she smelled when he walked in the door, and the smear of lipstick on his neck. He stood with an absolute emotionless expression; like he did not have to answer her or like she wasn't even there.

First she was angry and hurt that he would dismiss her this way. She tried so hard to keep him satisfied and this is how he treated her? Then she started to cry from overwhelming frustration and anger. But the longer she stood looking at him; she began to feel fear for this man that stood in front of her in his inexpressive way. She had never seen him act like this.

As she stared at his blank expression, like magic, the curtains on her eyes opened and Neil did not look like the treasure she had thought he had been. He looked ugly as he staggered and leaned on the wall next to the kitchen. He was unkempt with a torn shirt and cowboy boots covered with mud. He needed a haircut and it looked like he had not shaven for days. He looked spiteful with bloodshot eyes and he stood in a superior manner towards her.

As she observed him with newly opened eyes, she wondered how he planned on taking care of her when he did not take care of himself. She wondered how she did not see him like this yesterday or the day before that. She suddenly felt dirty and used.

Jenna knew she had to get out and turned to head out the door. She screamed, "I'm done with you!"

Just as she went to open the door, he grabbed her arm and swung her around. Her arm felt like it had been torn from its socket and the sudden pain filled her eyes with tears. Shocked and terrified, she turned and saw a haunting look in his eyes that she'd never seen. She was afraid.

"You are nothing without me!" he had screamed into her face. The smell of alcohol was stifling on his breath and slobber filled the corners of his mouth. He pushed her back and then pushed her back again, this time with brutal force. "No one will ever want someone like you, NO ONE!"

Jenna hit hard against the door frame that had led to the bathroom. For a brief moment, it knocked the breath from her. He grabbed her shoulders and kicked her feet out from under her with one swift stroke of his boot. Then she was on the floor. Before she could even move he was on top of her. His hands were around her neck with immense force. He was screaming into her face but she could not hear him through the pounding sound in her ears.

Suddenly, his hateful eyes showed fear for just one second, like he had been slapped. He took his hand from the back of her neck and raised it in front of his face. It was covered with blood, her blood. Her head had hit the door frame with such force that it had fractured her skull.

Then just as quickly, his expression, which had been fear, evaporated into absolute detachment again. Immediately he stood up and stepped over her and walked into the bathroom, where he grabbed some towels. He used one towel to soak up the blood from the floor and gave her a towel for her head, all without saying a word. Then he did the most peculiar thing. First, he handed her a fresh towel for her head, and took the blood-soaked one from her. Next, he grabbed the other towel, from the floor, and went to the washing machine. He put the blood-soaked towels into the machine, with some detergent, and started the washer. Finally, he walked to the refrigerator and opened the door and looked inside. Like it was any other day, he commented that there was nothing to eat and asked when she was going to go to the store for groceries.

At that moment, as Jenna sat holding the towel to the back of her head, she knew this man was beyond anything she had imagined. She needed to get out, or she felt he would kill her and she was not going to be another victim of domestic abuse.

Her feet felt numb from the shock of what had just happened, but somehow she made them move and ran for the door. As she threw the door open, she heard heavy footsteps running after her. Without looking back she ran to the neighbors' and desperately banged on the door, praying that they were home. Still terrified, she was afraid to look back, but she quickly glanced behind her and could see him disappear, as a shadow, under the light of the porch, back into the house.

Jenna opened her eyes and felt tears streaming down her face. She wiped the tears off her cheeks as she looked around her backyard and almost expected Neil to appear from behind a tree or bush.

The whole relationship had left her scarred physically and mentally and she had trouble forming relationships because of it. Even after five years, she was scared to get close to another man because she feared the worst from any man she met. She feared she would never be able to trust another man again.

She wished she could call her mom to feel better but then thought about all the mistakes that had been made and how all of this had affected her relationship with her family. She grinded her teeth and was in turmoil with herself when she thought about what she had done to her family. She was so disappointed with herself and still could not believe she had let another person change her like Neil had. But shortly into their relationship, Jenna had begun to resent her whole family for not falling in love with him like she had. At that time, she thought he was the perfect man and could not believe that they did not see it too. She would look at her family with disgust and began to see them as the enemy.

Then, when they tried to intervene and get her away from Neil, Jenna said hurtful, degrading words before she slammed the door to her parents' home and left forever. She had walked to her car, which Neil was waiting in, and had seen a look of accomplishment on his face. And as she had closed her car door, she looked back at the house and saw her parents' looking at her with hurt and worry. Now years later, she still did not know what to say to them or her siblings. She did not know how to apologize for her harsh words and could never believe they would forgive her.

Wiping her eyes again with the back of her hand, Jenna looked down at Shadow sleeping peacefully on her lap. She felt his soft hair and could feel his heartbeat against her hand. She tried to concentrate on this, and only this, and pushed the bad memories back to the furthest place in her mind.

Jenna took a deep breath and got up from her chair. She knew it was time for her to get to work on her pictures. It was a good way to forget her past, at least for a while.

After entering the house and locking the door behind her, Shadow went to his doggy bed and dozed again within seconds. Jenna sat down at her computer to download the pictures from the day at the beach. As the pictures began to move from the camera to the computer she was amazed how many she had taken without realizing it. Thankful for new technology, she was glad she had a digital camera since she would be broke if she had to buy the film from all the extra pictures she had taken. Her camera was not the newest or most expensive camera out there, but it worked well and her clients were happy with the work she did.

Jenna glanced at a few of the pictures as they transferred to her computer and instantly knew taking so many had paid off. The people's expressions were amazing. She couldn't stop the smile from crossing her lips.

From the goofy face to the serious and from artful to angry, she had captured it all. The pictures displayed a child's joy as he put a seashell at the top of his completed castle and a man's rage as his sand dragon collapsed under the pressure of the wet sand. Jenna admired countless other pictures and thought it had been a delight to capture it all with her lens.

It made her happy that she had chosen a profession that she adored and not one just for the amount of money she would make. She enjoyed being at the right place and the right time to capture an emotion that otherwise would never be seen or remembered. But now, she had the tedious task of cropping and fine-tuning the hundreds of pictures she had taken.

After a few hours of working on the pictures, something caught her eye. "No way!" she gasped as she cropped the picture closer. She had captured the man from the diner in one of her pictures. How could that be? She didn't see him the entire day until the diner.

Jenna began to look through other pictures and found there was more than one. She saw there were numerous pictures of the man. She felt her heart flutter again as she looked at him.

As she scoured the pictures, she saw that he looked the same as when she had seen him at the diner, except for the pink cheeks and sweat showing through his shirt. It was obvious he had never seen a competition like this before and the expressions on his face were priceless.

She couldn't take her eyes off the pictures of him. He looked good and photographed well. She exhaled with satisfaction as she examined his face. But just as fast, she felt a moment of dread that he, like Neil, in the past, would end up abusing her. She hated to feel this way but it always seemed to be embedded into her subconscious and there didn't seem to be a way to escape it. Jenna shook her head and tried to push the thought away and looked through the countless pictures for more images of him.

She ended up finding eight pictures total with the man. Not the best quality photos, since he was not the main attraction, but he was still there. She grinned.

Jenna got lost in the pictures of him. She memorized every expression and couldn't believe he had been there. She felt warmth run through her body as she admired his grin.

Shaking her head, she frowned. "What am I doing? He's not the job and I need to get to it," she said.

Impulsively, she printed the pictures to save for herself. She looked at them one last time and then put them to the bottom of a pile of photos to hide them from herself.

# chapter 4

THE NEXT COUPLE of days seemed a blur. Jenna spent endless time sitting in front of the computer, cropping and editing pictures, until it was finally complete. It would be hours before she would get up to eat, let Shadow out, stretch, or sleep. But that is what she had to do to get the job done. Finally, she printed the pictures and looked at her work. She knew it was good.

Pictures had always been an easy way to express her personality. Since she was young she could tell a story with her portrayals and people would feel the emotion she had captured. After years of practice she knew how to make pictures stand out and she had a good eye for detail. It was everything else she had a hard time expressing herself with. The other aspects of her life were difficult, but pictures seemed effortless.

She placed the majority of the pictures in the portfolio and put them in an envelope to be mailed. Keeping a few for herself, she rolled her shoulders to try and release some of the tension. She let out a satisfied breath and pushed away from the desk. It was time for a break and she couldn't wait to get outside into the fresh air and move. It was a beautiful day for a walk so she headed to the beach to stretch her legs.

After a short drive Jenna and Shadow were splashing in the waves. Then as she sat on the beach, she let the sand warm her feet and the sun warm her skin. Every few seconds the tide brought salty water up past her knees and she felt free again.

Jenna relaxed on her oversized beach towel and soaked in the afternoon sunshine while Shadow dug a hole in the warm sand to lie in the cool sand underneath. She breathed in the ocean air and still couldn't believe, after five years, she was living in Maryland. She felt this was where she was supposed to be. It was home.

But as the cool breeze began to float towards them from the waves she knew it was time to pack up and head back home. She gathered up her beach bag and belongings and decided to head to the diner for dinner first. She always felt special when she was with Kathy and John and right now she craved that attention.

As they got closer to the diner, the usual tug on the leash reminded Jenna of when they had been there last. She thought of the man who made her heart flutter and later had appeared in her pictures. As they sat down at Jenna's favorite table, she got a warm sensation throughout her body just thinking about him.

"Well, hello there, stranger," she heard a deep gruff voice say behind her.

She turned to see John. His salt and pepper hair fit his character perfectly. He had the body of a lumberjack but the personality of a teddy bear. His smile always brought a sparkle to his blue-gray eyes and his voice was rough like an old cowboy off the open range. Every day he wore overall bibs with a white shirt like a farmer and steel-toed boots like a construction worker. He was in his mid-sixties, like Kathy, but didn't act like he was ready to retire anytime soon. He felt like a father figure to her but sometimes he seemed more like a grandpa or a friend.

"Where you been?" He asked. "Kathy said you took off abruptly after being smitten with a good-looking young man," he said as he smirked and winked at Jenna.

Jenna felt her face get warm and looked away embarrassed. She remembered how she had left to escape the situation and how it had felt to be close to him. "Oh, you know. I had to get to my pictures and I was on a deadline. I did get done, by the way, and just so you know I was not smitten with the guy." She began to fumble with her hands in her lap and wanted the conversation about that day to be over. "I just got done with my pictures earlier this afternoon. There were some really good ones."

"Uh-huh," he said as he disappeared back inside the diner with a grin on his face.

From inside the door Jenna could hear Kathy whisper and scold John. Jenna heard her say "That was supposed to be a secret." Then she heard John's laugh fade as he headed back to the kitchen.

"I'm sorry about that," Kathy said as she brought out the usual lemonade and bowl of water with ice cubes. "He doesn't understand after forty years, that pillow talk is supposed to stay on the pillow."

"Oh, don't worry about it. I left like a little girl with a school crush. I was mad at you at first but then I didn't care. It was all silly. I don't know why I got so flustered."

Kathy put her hand on Jenna's and stood in front of her, casting a large shadow with the setting sun behind her. "I know what it was but you won't admit it." She sighed and looked at the diner's exterior. "You need to let those walls down around your heart sometime, sweetie. Even just a little so you can feel what you are missing. I know your past has left you scarred but not all men are that way." She sat in a chair next to Jenna's and looked inside the diner door. "Look at my John. Most people cower when they see him but he is as gentle as any man I've met. You know how it was. You were intimidated of him when you first met but after he talked to you for a while you realized what a good soul he is. The point is that you can't judge a book by its cover. If you don't open the book, you'll never know the story on the inside. Some stories *do* turn out good Jenna. I've been blessed to find my soul mate and we both want you to find that someone special too."

Jenna didn't know how to answer her. She knew she kept her heart well-guarded but she wasn't ready to let down any wall yet. She was scared if she allowed a man into her life that he would mistreat her.

She knew there were good men out in the world, but didn't know if she would choose the right one. She didn't know if she was strong enough to see the warning signs. And if she did, she didn't know if she could end the relationship. It had taken something horrible for her to finally end the last one and was scared what it would take if it happened again. It was better to be single right now.

Kathy looked at her. "Okay dear, I'll quit. I can see when I'm on the losing end of a fight. What do you and Shadow want to dine on this evening?"

Jenna looked around the other tables of customers and saw plates with scallops, crab, and burgers. She felt her stomach grumble. She had been so busy with the pictures that her appetite had diminished while working. Now, as she looked and smelled the food surrounding her, her appetite was back. Her mouth was salivating. She ordered some food for herself and watched as Kathy pushed a strand of hair back from her face.

Jenna put her hands in her lap and felt like a confused child. "I'll think about what you said."

Kathy turned around and walked through the door of the diner to get the food order. "All right, sounds good to me."

As Kathy walked away Jenna pondered on what Kathy meant. Was her last comment about the food or about her walls being up around her heart?

# chapter 5

JENNA DROVE ALONG the highway to get to her next photo job. She started to think about what Kathy had said a couple days before and questioned it. What if Kathy was right and she was wasting the time she had on this earth living without a good man in her life? Did she need that kind of companionship to be happy? What if she did get into a relationship and it started good and turned horrible like Neil? What if … "

BAM!

"Oh hell, now what?" she whined to herself and pulled over to the side of the road. Moaning, she got out of the car and discovered a flat tire on the driver's side. "Of all days to have this happen, what do I do now?" She raised her hands in the air in defeat.

She was supposed to be at the fairgrounds in less than an hour and was already running late. Kicking the gravel beside the road, she walked to the trunk and kicked at the flat tire as she walked by it. She popped the trunk open and grabbed a spare, a jack, and a tire iron.

"So much for me looking professional. I'm going to be a sweaty, dirty mess by time I get there," she complained to herself.

Jenna grunted as she tried to loosen the lug nuts. They were tight on the rim and there was no way she was going to loosen them herself. She cursed under her breath at the same time she heard a car door open and close.

A man's deep voice behind her said, "You need some help?"

Startled, Jenna stood up before she wiped the dirt off her knees. She turned around and about collapsed and leaned back on her car for support.

The man in front of her was the same man from the diner. He was the same man who she had found in the photos she had taken at the sandcastle competition. She tried to catch her breath and avoided his gaze. "Thank you, but I can call a friend."

He leaned down next to the flat tire. "Well, you're a ways from town and I'm here now, so why don't I take care of this for you?"

Before Jenna could object he grabbed the tire iron and had one lug nut loose. She stood next to her car and didn't know what to do or say. She watched as his arms flexed effortlessly to jack up the car, remove the lug nuts and then replace the tire with the spare.

She could smell his cologne as it wafted on the light breeze and felt intoxicated by it and then she felt like her feet were stuck in cement. She couldn't move if she had wanted to.

She couldn't tell if she was scared or not scared of the man in front of her. Her emotions seemed to be jumbled and she was lost for words. She wanted to tell him to go away but in the same instant she did not want him to go anywhere. She could not take her eyes off him, feeling desire for him, but felt like she was trapped in time.

He casually took the ruined tire and placed it in the trunk with the jack and tire iron. Flexing his arms he slammed the trunk shut and turned towards Jenna. "See, I'm all done before you could even make that call," he said and smiled before leaning back on the car beside her. "By the way, I'm Keith," he added and wiped his hands on his blue jeans before he extended his right hand out.

Jenna extended her hand out and felt her cell phone in the palm of it. She didn't even know that she had even taken it out of her purse. Quickly, she shook Keith's hand, and then put her hands into the pockets of her skirt as she looked down at the ground.

He backed away from the car. "I didn't mean to push myself on you. I can put the other tire back on if it will make you more comfortable. I just wanted to help out," he said and pointed to the trunk of her car.

Jenna saw his confusion and cursed under her breath. She needed to quit being so shy and guarded. It was a bad combination.

"I'm sorry. I really appreciate the help," she said softly and kicked the spare tire surprised that she could move. "I'm being rude. You've been so kind and I'm not being very nice. I'm Jenna. Thank you for helping me out of a jam," she said.

Keith leaned back on her car again. "Hey it was no problem. I've changed quite a few tires so it was no trouble at all." His brow wrinkled like he was trying to think back. "Hey, didn't I see you a few days ago at that diner on the boardwalk? I think your hair was back in a braid on that day and you had some flour on your face." He tilted his head to look in the car and tried to peer into the windows. "Yeah, you had a little white dog with you too."

Jenna had hoped he wouldn't recollect that day but was impressed he remembered so many details. "Yep, that was me," she said, sighing. "It's a great place and the owners, Kathy and John, are good people. I tend to go there a lot," she added, but then regretted giving him so much information. She cursed under her breathe again and wondered what was wrong with her. She didn't act this way or even talk to men unless she absolutely had to.

"So where's the pup at?" he asked as he looked back into the car window and seemed to want to prolong the conversation.

Jenna just stood there and could not speak scared she would say more than she should.

Not getting a response he backed away. "Well Jenna, it was very nice to meet you again. Did you need anything else?"

"No, no, I'm good. I really need to get going." She pointed down the highway and took a step back. "I'm late for an appointment."

Keith folded his arms in front of him and wrinkled his forehead. "Hmm, I think it was an appointment that you had to leave for the last time too. You sure are a busy person. What is it that you do?" he asked and watched her chew on her bottom lip nervously.

Jenna put her hand on her hip and looked towards her car. She felt she had already said too much and needed to get away. "Well, I do a lot of things and I need to get to it."

Keith smiled and let out a small laugh. "Oh, lots of things. I hear that line of work is very time consuming."

His voice made her heart skip a beat and his hazel eyes drew her to him. He was about a foot taller than she was, but she didn't care. She liked tall men but definitely hadn't been thinking about any, or looking for that matter. If anything, she was trying to avoid men as much as possible.

His arms were crossed in front of him and she wondered how it would feel to have his strong arms around her. She pushed the thought away and felt foolish. "I'm a photographer. I need to be at the fairgrounds and I really am late," she responded quickly.

"Well that explains why you don't have your pup with you. I'll let you get to it then. It really was nice to meet you again Jenna. Hopefully we bump into each other again sometime," he said and dug his hands into his pockets.

"I would like that." Jenna said and was surprised when she heard the words escape her lips.

Keith stood up straight. "Really? Great! How about getting some lunch tomorrow back at that diner?"

Jenna didn't know how to answer. Confused, she didn't even know why she said she wanted to see him again. She started to walk towards her car door and tried to think at the same time. They would be around Kathy and John, so it should be all right. But what if … "Yes, that would be all right I guess," she answered him and watched for his reaction.

Keith started to walk towards his SUV as he spoke "Great, I'll see you around twelve thirty tomorrow. Bye, Jenna." He quickly stepped inside and drove away.

Jenna watched the dust settle on the road behind him and wondered why she had agreed to have lunch with him. She swore he practically ran to his vehicle so she couldn't change her mind. Did he know she might have?

Jenna looked down the road one more time and her thoughts were flooded with Keith's image. She wondered why he had been there. Was it a coincidence or was it fate? There seemed to be a lot of unanswered questions about him but, right now, she had to get down the road to the fairgrounds. Smiling, she got into her car and shook her head and couldn't believe it had happened. "Life's full of surprises," was all she could say as she headed down the road.

# chapter 6

THE HOURS JENNA waited for the lunch date were excruciating. She braided her hair and put on some small earrings. That was the most she was going to do, along with her red sundress, since she didn't want Keith to think she was trying too hard and was still confused why she agreed to meet him for lunch in the first place.

Walking up to the diner was difficult and she rubbed her hands together nervously. Over the years she had walked here countless times, but today was different. As she got closer to the diner, she scanned the tables, from far off, but she couldn't tell if he was there or not.

Kneeling down momentarily, Jenna felt the soft hair on Shadow's back. She was happy that Shadow was with her for comfort. But he pulled on the leash impatiently and was tired of staying in one place.

Shadow pulling her was the only way she got to the destination without turning around and running home. She had mixed emotions of excitement to see Keith, but also had the intuition to try and protect herself, to run away.

She took a few more steps to be closer to the diner, took a deep breath, and looked at the umbrella-covered tables. All the tables were occupied, even her favorite one. The people sitting there were still wet from playing in the ocean and had sunburns that were really going to hurt when the sun went down.

The whole family had strawberry blonde hair and the way they acted, they had never been to a beach like this before. They behaved like they were out of place and were hyper, especially the children. Their eyes darted around as they tried to take in all the scenery and none of them seemed to be used to the busy atmosphere. But it was good to see people so happy and she was all right with them sitting at the table she preferred.

Biting her bottom lip, Jenna looked around at the other tables, but did not see Keith's hazel eyes anywhere. She felt let down but couldn't figure out why. This was good news, wasn't it? Maybe he wouldn't show up today or any day and she wouldn't have to see him again. Why did she feel deflated? Jenna took a deep breath and looked at her watch. It was almost one o'clock. She had been standing in one place, wasting time. She was late but she didn't see Keith so it didn't matter. Maybe he had forgotten about the lunch date all together.

She pushed the thought of being stood up from her mind and decided to go into the diner to get a bite to eat to take home. There was no reason that she would have to go home hungry. And that way if he showed up late he would not see her and she would not have to deal with the situation.

Jenna glanced at all the people one more time to make sure she hadn't missed Keith and stepped inside. As her eyes adjusted to the darker environment, she glanced around the interior of the diner.

The colors were tan and green with fake plants placed sporadically around the area. It was small inside with a few stools next to the counter and it smelled like seafood and burgers mixed with the faint smell of pastries. It was considerably old but she could tell that they had made improvements over the years to try and keep it looking good.

Behind the counter Jenna saw that Kathy was talking to John through the little opening in the wall where he placed the food orders for customers. Kathy's hair was in the usual bun and she was wearing blue capris with a pink t-shirt with a flamingo on the back. John had on a green baseball cap with a crab on the front, smiling at Kathy with a sparkle in his eyes. Jenna watched them and could feel the love between them. She wondered if she would ever feel love like theirs' and it made her curious about what they were talking about.

Shadow let out a small whimper as he sat next to Jenna's legs. John promptly looked up when he heard the noise and smiled.

Kathy turned around and then winked at Jenna. "Well, hello there, Jenna and Shadow. How are my favorite customers doing today?"

Jenna slouched. "We're doing okay, I guess," she said but decided against telling Kathy about Keith standing her up. "I just thought Shadow and I would get a bite to eat to take home with us."

Kathy looked at Jenna confused. She wrinkled her forehead and put her hands on her hips and gestured to the table behind Jenna with a nod of her head. "Well, what about the gentleman behind you? Isn't he going to eat with you too?"

Jenna's body went numb and she could feel the color drain from her face. She felt like her feet were on a turntable as she rotated slowly towards the table behind her. Looking towards the wall, connecting to the door she had just entered, she saw that Kathy and John had set up a card table with a couple of chairs next to the window. They had placed a plastic table cloth on it and added a lit candle too. And, at the table, sitting patiently, Keith sat with his hands folded and feet crossed down below with a grin on his face. His smile grew bigger as she looked over at him and met his gaze.

Jenna fumbled for words and felt her face get warm. "Oh. I didn't even … I didn't even look behind me when I came in." Jenna felt embarrassed and wanted to run away. Kathy gripped her arm and gently led her to the table and Jenna reluctantly sat down.

Kathy explained. "Keith came into the diner earlier and said he was going to meet you here for lunch. We were pretty surprised. John and I didn't want him to miss it, since it is the busiest time of day, I'm sure you know. So we went and retrieved the table and chairs from the old shed out back. Hope you both enjoy the meal." Kathy squeezed Jenna's shoulder softly. She whispered, "You're running a little late aren't you Jenna? I'd hope that you didn't take your time on purpose." Kathy didn't wait for an answer and grabbed Shadow's leash from Jenna's hand. "I'll tie Shadow outside for you so you can have a nice lunch with no more distractions."

Jenna watched Kathy as she went out the door with Shadow and felt like her armor had just been stripped from her. Suddenly alone, she felt like a shy little kid sitting in church with people she didn't know. Trying not to think about it, she turned back to the table and looked down at the pattern of dolphins swimming on the table cloth. She did not want to look up and was extremely uncomfortable. She felt like she had been caught off guard and thrown into a situation she was not prepared for.

Keith watched Jenna's expression. "Didn't you think I was going to be here? I don't miss lunch dates." He joked. "They're the best kind to have." He watched her examine the table cloth like it was a piece of art work. "Are you okay?" he asked with no response to his question.

Jenna looked up from the table cloth and saw both John and Kathy glance over at her like worried parents. She couldn't tell if this comforted her or made her more nervous. Trying to make the best of the situation, she tried to not look nervous but didn't do a very good job. First she spilled her lemonade on the table and then she knocked her silverware on the floor trying to clean up the lemonade with a napkin.

Kathy was smiling as she brought a towel to help clean up the mess. She patted Jenna's hand, "It's okay. I just made a fresh pitcher a minute ago. I'll get you a fresh glass."

Jenna glanced at Keith and then looked down again. She dabbed some lemonade off her red dress and felt her face turn just as red. "I've always been a klutz. I've had more banged-up knees and bruises than anyone I know."

"It's fine. Really, please stop being so nervous. I'm not going to ask you to marry me."

Sarcastically she said, "Well we can't get married yet. I haven't met your parents or even know your last name. We're not in Vegas, mister."

He raised his eyebrows for a second. "Wow! There's the spitfire I was sure was in you!"

Jenna started to get a knot in her stomach and knew she shouldn't have come. She felt the same as she had with every man before this, a feeling that she would be trapped and would not be able to get away if she let her guard down and let another man get close to her. Suddenly she wished she'd stayed home. "Why'd you want to meet anyway? There are a lot of women around here. Why'd you pick me? Am I an easy target?"

Keith leaned back in his chair and crossed his arms, "An easy what?" he paused. "Jenna, I simply find you alluring and thought we could talk a little," he said. "I don't want to make you uncomfortable. I did notice the other women but none of them caught my attention like you did," he said sympathetically. "If you want me to go, I'll go and not come back. I'm not holding you hostage or trying to get anything from you but conversation. I'm sorry if you saw anything beyond that. I'm not that kind of guy. I'm sorry if you got that impression although I don't know how you would." He put his hands on the table and folded them and his knuckles turned white. He looked out the window towards the ocean.

Jenna was suddenly embarrassed from what she said and watched him stare out the window. "No, I want you to stay. You're right. I need to relax. A little conversation won't hurt us. I don't know why I ... " she watched Keith as she spoke and he didn't react to her words and continued to stare out the window. She gave up trying to explain herself. She felt foolish and hated how her past seemed to control her actions now even after five years.

Kathy interrupted the silence a few minutes later with a feast of sautéed shrimp and fresh steamed crab.

Jenna watched as Kathy spread newspaper on top of the dolphin tablecloth and then she dumped two dozen steamed crab on top of the newspaper. She set the shrimp to the side and refilled both of their glasses with lemonade. She gave them each silverware to crack the crabs open and pull the meat out. Then she gave them each a bib with a crab on the front of it before she walked back to kitchen with John. She had not said a word the entire time and Jenna thought that Kathy could tell that there was tension between her and Keith. As Kathy walked away a smirk crossed Jenna's face and she thought it might be fun to watch Keith eat crab.

Keith turned as Kathy brought the food to the table and tucked a napkin into the neck of his shirt, ignoring the bib. He grabbed a crab before he let out a sigh. "How do you eat these things?"

Jenna giggled and felt more at ease. She began to show Keith the proper way to open fresh crab and how to get the most meat from the legs and the claws like Kathy had taught her. Then she showed him how to get meat from the rest of the body and watched his face as he dipped the meat into melted butter and took his first bite.

Keith's eyes got wide. "WHOA!" He sucked the juice and butter from his fingers and dug in for some more. "This is awesome! Fresh seafood is the best. I could sit here all day eating this. I've been here for a week and I can't believe I haven't tried this yet."

Jenna smiled and watched him. She liked the napkin in his shirt and butter on the bottom of his chin. It reminded her of when she was in high school and brought home a date for dinner. If her parents hadn't met the date, they would have a big plate of spaghetti and meatballs, with extra sauce and cheese, in front of him. That was their way of seeing how he would behave in the situation. Jenna looked at Keith and she knew he would pass her parents' test with flying colors. She ate some shrimp and a couple crabs then sat back and watched Keith gorge himself on the crabmeat.

After opening a dozen crabs, Keith finally got his fill and threw an empty crab shell on the table. "Okay." He grabbed a wet nap and opened it to get the butter from his face. "I have to quit or I'm going to have to undo my belt and pants. I don't think that would make a very good first impression with you."

Jenna laughed and realized that was something she hadn't done in a long time with a guy, except for John of course. Her cheeks actually hurt from smiling so much. She hadn't had a day like this for a long time, and it felt good.

After Keith cleaned up, he took the napkin from his shirt and laughed, "If you're not wearing a napkin, it's not good food." He paused. "This has been fun. I'm glad you showed up, even a little late, so I could fill my belly," he said and tapped his stomach with his hands then pushed back from the table. "You want to go for a walk with me and walk off some of this food?"

"I'd like that." Jenna said. She stood up and glanced at Kathy who had a smile on her face and held her hands to her heart. "Thank you," Jenna said directing her attention towards Kathy and gave her a kiss on the cheek.

They walked out of the diner, adjusted their eyes to the brightness of the sunshine and were greeted by a very excited dog. Jenna untied his leash and strolled towards the beach. "Let's go for a walk, Shadow." Shadow happily trotted on one side of her and Keith walked on the other.

It felt natural for Jenna to walk with Keith. He was comfortable to be around and she was scared by that fact, but it seemed to fade as they walked. She hadn't felt comfortable around another man in years.

They stepped off the boardwalk and out onto the beach. When Jenna's feet touched the sand, she took off her sandals and let the warmth caress her feet. Keith did the same. When the sand touched his bare feet he made a funny face and Jenna giggled to herself. She shook her head and directed her attention to the beach.

It was busy with families building sandcastles together and children chasing the waves. There were couples lying on beach towels engaged in conversations and others beginning to pack up to return to their hotel or home. Jenna raised her face to the sky and felt the heat penetrate her skin. The warmth from the sun felt good against her and being next to Keith made her feel even warmer. She needed to cool the sensations her body was developing and wanted to run to the ocean to dive into its chilly water. Deciding against it, Jenna looked at Keith and wondered if he felt the same about her. "Well, Keith, tell me a little about you."

Keith picked up a few seashells and started to examine them. "Where do I start? Well, let's see. I was born and raised in Iowa, as an only child, and my folks are still there today. I played football in college and went to school to be a computer geek. I guess that's what you would call me. I had an opportunity to transfer here to take over a senior web developer position with a company here in town. I guess I felt this could be a different scene from all the cornfields, so I took it. I moved here a while ago so I could have time to get to know my surroundings a little. I don't know my way around too much but I can get to the bank, grocery store, my apartment and the beach. That's enough to get me by for now. And in all that time I've never been barefoot in the sand or had a fresh crab. Thanks for the opportunity." He threw a seashell back into the ocean it just came from. "That about sums it up."

Jenna snickered. "You're welcome for lunch. I thought it was pretty good too, although I was a little late. So you're a senior web developer? Sounds like an interesting job. What are you going to do there?"

"I'm actually going to help with designing technical solutions and recognizing system problems and fixing them. I'll be leading a group, which I'm not sure they'll like it or not coming from me. A bunch of other technical jargon and I'm assuming a lot of pressure. So a little vacation before I started sounded good, and meeting you even made it better. How about you?" he asked and shuffled his bare feet in the sand to make a figure eight shape. "I know you are a photographer but what do you take pictures of?"

Jenna took a deep breath. "Wow, your job sounds a lot more difficult than mine. I take a lot of different kinds of pictures. I'm guess I'm still trying to get a feel for my photo personality, although I don't know if I ever will."

Keith chimed in, "I'm sure you outshine me. My pictures always crop out someone's head. Even if I use a digital camera the pictures come out blurry and never look right. It has always amazed me how I can take a picture and then someone who has an eye for it, can take the same picture and they end up looking totally different."

She smirked and imagined Keith taking pictures of models and all their heads being cropped out. "Well, it's more than just taking pictures. I have to submit a bid to get the job and after I get it I have to get photo releases from any people involved. Then I have to copyright my work. Sometimes I have to hire a model, which is the good part about living right next to a beach with beautiful women and men walking around every day. If anything, that's the easiest part. Although I hire women more than I ever hire men."

"I'm looking at a very beautiful lady right now," Keith said as he gazed into her eyes. "I've never seen green eyes like yours. They're gorgeous."

Jenna could feel her cheeks get warm and she felt embarrassed. She looked away and glanced down at Shadow. His nose was now covered with wet sand as he dug through it to chase after something below. "Shadow, you definitely should've been born a different color," she said and bent down to try to wipe the sand from his nose while trying to change the subject.

Keith bent down so he was eye level with her. "Why do you call him Shadow? That intrigued me when you first said his name."

Jenna kept looking at Shadow and scratched him behind the ears. "Well, when I got Shadow, he was just a little puppy. I didn't know what I was going to name him. I had thought of fluffy or sugar but I decided to wait on the name until it was just right. So that night I put him in a basket for our first night together and he whined the whole time I had him there. I mean, from the second his little paws hit the bottom of the basket to the time I picked him back up. It really only was about five minutes but it felt like hours. It drove me crazy. So after a few minutes he ended up lying in bed with me. The next morning, as I tried to get dressed, I about tripped over him a dozen times. Every time I turned around he was right behind me … just like a shadow."

"Hmm, that makes sense. Whenever I had a pet it was Fido or Max. I never tried to fit the personality to the dog. You're pretty amazing," he said as he reached to touch Jenna's cheek.

She pulled away and stood up. She was instantly frustrated that her past was winning again. She could not even enjoy a simple touch without fear entering her mind. "Well, time has certainly gone by fast. Better call it a day, don't you think? I'm sure you have unpacking to do or grocery shopping or something."

"Oh … okay," Keith said and looked puzzled. "I guess I've more unpacking to do. I have a couple more days until I have to start at work." He scratched behind Shadow's ears and then stood up. "Would you want to do something tomorrow?"

"Sure," Jenna squeaked out before she knew she had even answered.

"Could I get your number to set it up?"

She rattled off her number at her house and wondered if he would remember it without writing it down. She put Shadow's leash back on and started to back away.

"Well then, have a good rest of the day," Keith said.

Jenna turned to leave and couldn't shake the feeling that he was not the kind of guy to be afraid of. "Okey dokey,"

She headed to her car with Shadow and glanced back to see Keith standing in the sand gazing at the ocean. She wondered what he was thinking about and hoped she hadn't scared him away but she was so hesitant when a man tried to get close to her. Would she ever be able to break those walls down to let someone in?

# chapter 7

TAKING A SHOWER, Jenna had the phone on the vanity so she wouldn't miss it if it rang. She couldn't decide if she was excited for Keith to call or scared if he would, but she needed the phone close by to decide. After her shower, when she dried her hair, she shut the hairdryer off twice because she thought she heard the phone ring. Each time she shook her head in annoyance before starting the hairdryer again. Shortly after, she dressed in shorts and a tank top and went outside to water her flowers, with the cordless phone close by.

Shadow jumped at the spraying water and tried to catch it but soon grew bored with the activity. He wandered off under a tree to take a nap. Jenna took a break too and sat down in a chair next to him. "Shadow, why did I give him my house phone number instead of my cell phone? No one calls the house phone but telemarketers and I was going to disconnect it. Now I feel like I can't do anything because I need to stay by the phone. I really wasn't thinking. I shouldn't have given him my number at all."

Shadow looked up at her as she spoke and cocked his head side to side like he was trying to understand what she was saying.

"Okay, I'll give him two more hours to call then you and I will take off and go for a car ride. Sound good?"

Shadow started panting and then he laid his head down and closed his eyes.

"Well, I guess I'm done talking to you then fur ball."

Jenna got up and busied herself watering flowers before going inside to do some dishes and tidy up the kitchen. All the while she kept the phone within arm's reach. As she dried the last dish, she looked at the clock and it seemed it was moving slower than it ever had before. She threw the towel on the counter and stormed off to the living room. "This is crazy!" she said to herself. "I've been waiting on a man to call like a little girl with an infatuation. I need to get out of here for a while."

She grabbed her camera and Shadow and headed to the car. As they walked, she cursed under her breath the whole time for waiting around instead of enjoying the day. "We'll find some good pictures to take for my portfolio, and then get some pizza, but I better grab a hat," she said to Shadow and ran back to the house. Just as she was went to shut the door to leave again, the phone rang. Her heart started to pound so hard, she could hear it in her ears.

"Hello?"

"Hey, Jenna, am I calling at a good time?"

Jenna's heart thumped even harder. "Keith? Hi there. I didn't know if you would call."

"Of course I would. Are you still willing to do something? I don't really know what to do; this is more your territory, but I'm up for options."

She twirled her hair around her fingers and felt nervous. "Well sure. We, I mean Shadow and I, were just going out to take some pictures. You want to ride along?"

"That sounds good. Then I can see you do your magic. No pressure though."

"Yeah, no pressure. Where are you at? I can pick you up if you want? Or we can meet somewhere?"

"Well, if you're okay with it, why don't I meet you at your place? I want to drive around and learn the surroundings as much as possible. Will that work?"

Jenna got a knot in her stomach and didn't know if she wanted him to know where she lived. He seemed okay but she didn't really know him and he was a man. She knew she had to try and start trusting men at some point so she swallowed the fear rising in her throat and gave him her address and hung up. A few seconds later she got Shadow out of the car and brought him inside the house and looked at the clock. She figured it would take Keith fifteen minutes, depending on if he got lost or not. And she guessed he would get lost with the neighborhood she lived in. The streets twisted and turned and could get confusing.

Jenna walked towards her bedroom and decided to take Keith to a place other than the normal beach. She loved the beach by the boardwalk but she wanted to show him something that was different. She knew Shadow would have to be left behind but he didn't seem to care as long as he had a television on for the noise and chew bone to occupy him.

Actually feeling excited, Jenna went and put on her blue bikini along with a pink bathing suit cover up. She gathered her hair back into a ponytail and put on her pink flip flops with a large flower at the top of each foot. Finally, she grabbed a beach bag and included some towels, sunscreen, bottled water, and her camera and then waited.

Of course, she heard Keith's vehicle pull up to the house thirty minutes after they talked and she wondered how lost he had gotten but was not going to ask. After taking a deep breath, she opened the front door and felt her heart flutter when she saw him.

Keith was wearing blue and white swim trunks with a yellow t-shirt and flip flops. He smiled at her, put on his sunglasses, and posed beside his SUV just like a male model for a photo shoot.

Jenna started laughing and surprisingly felt at ease. She couldn't wait to spend the day with him. "Well, let's get going. I have the perfect place to take you."

Deciding to take Jenna's dark green colored Charger, Keith immediately started to talk about the valves, tires, and horse power. Jenna rolled her eyes and thought he sounded like her brother drooling over a car and it made her grin. She started the engine and heard Keith moan as she put the car into drive.

After a short drive they crossed a bridge and entered the parking lot of Jenna's favorite island not too far from where she lived. Jenna watched Keith's expression as she parked and ponies began to walk towards them looking for food. She could tell he was amazed, like she had been the first time, by the landscape and wild ponies walking around without fences to keep them enclosed. Jenna grabbed her bag and she and Keith walked down a trail to the beach.

The white sand, beneath Jenna's feet, felt warm and soft. The breeze made the grass on the dunes dance and the colors on the water sparkled. A few clouds moved slowly in the sky like molasses poured from a jar. The birds called to each other and sang just because they could. Tourists in boats floated by with the people taking pictures and beaming at each other as they watched dolphins jump from the water and eagles grab for a fish. It was a beautiful day and she was happy to have someone to share it with. They walked down to the shore and spread out some towels to sit down.

Keith looked around. "Wow. I didn't know there were places like this. The city is so busy. Even the beach is busy, and I assumed it was all like that. This is like a secret island. I can't get over it. I've never seen ponies without a fence holding them in or such awesome landscaping that is naturally made. Jenna, this is awesome."

"I discovered this place a couple years after I moved here. I was as fascinated as you are. I couldn't believe my luck to find this place. I've never brought anyone else here so this is a first for me. I usually come to take a few pictures and clear my head then leave." She paused a moment and then looked up at the sky. "There are so many types of birds around here. The common loon, bald eagles, purple sand pipers, and surf scooters depending on the time of year. I love watching them and did you know ... "

She was stopped in the middle of her sentence as Keith's hand turned her face and kissed her on the lips. His kiss was sensual and soft and it gave her arms goose bumps. He kept his hand on her face then moved it up and removed her ponytail holder so he could run his hand through her hair. At first her stomach tightened and she put her hands up to push him away but just as quickly she felt at ease and her arms went back to her sides. She relished the tenderness of his mouth.

His touch made her skin hot and she felt like currents of electricity were going throughout her entire body. His lips were warm and inviting and she moved closer to him as if she had no power to control herself. The world seemed to disappear and it was only Keith and her. Just as she moved her hand up to his face he backed away from her. She leaned back and looked at him with bewilderment and desire.

Keith smiled at her, stood up, took off his shirt and walked towards the water. "Well, let's go for a swim."

Jenna remained on the towel and was stunned. She could do nothing but watch him dive into the water. She had finally let a man near her and then he was the one who backed off. She thought it was funny and started to laugh. Amazingly, she did not even feel a little scared of him or the situation. She watched Keith splash the water and she pulled off her cover up and ran to the water too. When she reached it, she tackled Keith with the waves splashing around them and then Keith held her close. She felt the contrast of the cold water compared to the heat radiating from his body and liked it.

The cold water cooled her skin from his touch and she wanted more of the man next to her. As he stood up in the water and started to walk towards the shore, she tackled him again. He wasn't going to get away twice. They both fell and he laid in the wet sand with her on top of him, face to face. The waves pushed and pulled them with the current and she could feel his heart beat beneath her skin. She put her hand through his wet hair and gave a little tug. She pressed her lips to his. The warmth of his kiss compared to the cool water surrounding them was exhilarating. Memorizing every sensation, she felt his chest on her skin and his arms around her. It was perfect.

She kissed him passionately and felt him respond with the same intensity. She put her hands in his and then put his hands behind his head in the sand. He surrendered to what she did and she liked it that she was in control of the situation. She couldn't remember the last time she had control.

Closing her eyes, she saw a majestic swirl of colors and explosions behind her eyelids. The fire between them seemed unstoppable and his kisses got even more intense. It felt like they were in their own world and no one could ever come between them. But just as she thought this, a large shadow came over them and broke the spell.

Jenna looked up to see a foal looking down at them inquisitively. She started laughing and rolled onto the wet sand as the foal slowly walked away. She almost felt embarrassed that the ponies had been watching.

Keith stood up as he snickered and took her hand to help her up. "I guess we're not alone anymore." As he looked around he saw they were surrounded by more than a dozen ponies.

As the ponies lost interest and moved away from them, he walked to the beach towel, sat down to dry his body and watched as the ponies went towards some other people on the beach. "Well, that will always be a moment to remember," he said as he rifled through Jenna's beach bag. He pulled out her camera and fidgeted with it until he figured out how to turn it on. "I figured you brought a camera. This is a nice one. Hope I don't get sand in it," he said as he playfully threw it in the air and then aimed the lens at Jenna. "Say cheese."

Jenna smiled at him and knew no one had taken her picture for a long time. She had always been the one behind the lens, not very often in front of it.

"Let's see what you can do," she said and started to pose how she had seen the models pose for her.

She was confused being so relaxed with Keith but took advantage of the moment by enjoying it while it lasted. "Don't cut my head off in the picture," she said and she shook a finger at him.

Jenna started to dance around in the sand and gave many different poses before she ran to the water and dove in. She ducked her head under and held her breath for as long as her lungs would allow. When she came up for air she wiped her eyes and looked over at Keith. He had put the camera down and was staring at her. "What?" she asked.

"You are absolutely beautiful. Sorry if that makes you uncomfortable but, damn it, it's true."

She walked back to the towel and plopped down on her knees and then looked him in the eyes. "Tell me that again."

"You're beautiful Jenna."

She grazed his lips with the back of her hand and felt the urge to put her lips on his. "I like when you say that."

Jenna felt like her emotions were going wild. She had never felt this way with a man and she was confused yet excited. She did everything she could to not let the insecurities from her past trickle into her happy mood. But she needed to cool down her desires and regain her composure. Attempting to do just that, she grabbed her cover up, slipped it on and grabbed her camera from Keith's hands. "Give me a mean look."

Keith leaned back on the towel and supported himself on his elbows. He grinned.

Jenna took his picture and then frowned at him. "I said a mean look, not nice."

"I could never be mean to you. I can't even pretend."

Jenna's heart pounded hard in her chest and she felt a brick fall from the wall she had built around it. It wasn't as scary as she thought it would be and that terrified her. She needed to change the subject, and fast, before the moment would be ruined. "Okay, let's go take some pictures."

They walked down the shore and Jenna began to snap images. She took photographs of the ponies grazing, a bald eagle catching a fish, seagulls swaying on the wind currents, and a dolphin playing in the distance. She found some beautiful shells, watched a couple of children as they played Frisbee, and best of all, she couldn't stop smiling.

The sun was the perfect warmth, the breeze was the perfect flow, the birds sang the perfect songs, and Keith was the perfect person to spend the day with.

Keith pushed her hair behind her ear as they continued to stroll down the beach. "Can you tell me more about yourself than you take pictures?"

"Okay, like what?"

"Anything. I want to know the *real* Jenna."

Jenna felt her stomach do a somersault and felt her pulse quicken. She knew she was in new territory and pushed through the urge to run. She felt like she needed to find out where this day was going to lead them. "Let's see," she said as she tapped her pointer finger on her lips and tried to think of what to say. "I have one sister and one brother. One is older and one is younger than me. They both still live in Idaho along with my parents. Well, not with them, you know what I mean. Anyways, we were so close as kids and did everything together. I mean, if our parents' needed to find one of us, they would always find all three of us. We would be huddled over a puddle tossing in rocks or hiding under blankets we made into tents playing make-believe. The whole family would go camping or hiking and spend so much time looking up at the stars. We ate together, prayed together, and fought with each other." Jenna paused and took pleasure in the memories of her families' time together for a moment. She could remember it like it had all just happened yesterday. "But through it all we grew stronger and happier. My brother and sister and I were even close through the teenage years and spent as much time together as we could between sports and homework. And, of course, new crushes with other kids at school. We never hid secrets and knew everything that was going on in each other's lives." Jenna felt her stomach tighten and thought of Neil. "But then some stuff happened and I ruined it all. I needed to break away. This is where I ended up." Jenna slumped. "I'm not close to my family right now but that is another story altogether. I kind of feel like an outsider right now." She took a breath and looked out towards the water. "I've been here for five years and I got Shadow within the first month I moved into my house. So, I guess, he has experienced everything here with me. Then I met John and Kathy shortly after that. They are my family while I'm here. They've always been there for me and I hope I'm the same way for them."

She looked at her camera and smiled before she looked towards Keith to see if he was still listening. He was grinning at her and had an expression like he couldn't wait to hear what she had to say next. She felt pleased that he was giving her the attention she needed. "I guess I started taking pictures as a kid and knew right away that that was what I wanted to do when I grew up. You could say that I'm really awkward in situations with people. I'm sure you noticed. I don't ever know what to say or do and not too many people take the time to get to know who I really am. I guess they think I'm odd and I'll agree. I'm too self-conscious to put myself out there." Jenna examined one of the shells she had picked up from the sand. "I guess I figured out at a young age that people liked how I took pictures. They could see a side of me through my work. So, right then, I decided to do something people could relate to. It sure doesn't pay steady but I've gotten some pretty good contracts. And I guess since it's just being Shadow and I, it's enough. But it does help that I received an inheritance from my grandmother too. I dip into that if I really need to. In a nutshell, that's me." she said and shrugged her shoulders.

She continued to look at the shell in her hand and felt all of its contours. She could sense Keith beside her and she hoped he would not see her like other people did as strange or peculiar. She wanted him to take the time she needed to express who she was on the inside. She found it unusual but she really liked him and she wanted him to like her too. When she looked up she saw Keith looking at her with eager eyes.

He smiled and winked at her. "I want more. I want to know your favorite color and favorite food. How you looked as a teenager and if you had braces. I want to know all of it."

She fluttered her eyes at him playfully. "What fun would it be if I told you everything in one date?"

"You're right. That means I'll have to take you on a lot of dates to find out." His voice got quieter and Jenna had to lean towards him to hear his words. "You're a mystery and I feel like there is something dark in there. I feel like there is something that makes you hesitate when a guy tries to get close to you." Keith stopped walking and looked at the ground. "I don't know who he was but I already don't like him for hurting you that way." He glanced up at Jenna and had a serious expression. "Just know that I'll never harm you Jenna. I'll always try to make you smile." He grazed her cheek with the back side of his hand. "You've got a gorgeous smile."

Jenna felt tears welling up in her eyes and she fought them back. She had mixed emotions of joy that he wanted more time with her and scared that he already knew more about her than she thought he should. *How could he know her like this already?* It was like he could read her mind and that frightened her a lot. "I don't know anything about you, Keith, and you don't know me all that well. So why don't we stop this conversation so the day is not ruined. Please?"

"Sure thing. I don't want you running away, well because, you drove."

# chapter 8

JENNA FELT SCARED but also thrilled at the same time as she hung up the phone. She had not experienced too many baseball games throughout her life, but the thought of spending an afternoon at a ball field with Keith was exciting. She was proud of herself for pushing past those old feelings and trying to create new, good memories by asking Keith to go along with her.

Having a couple hours before they headed to the game, Jenna busied herself with washing her dishes and straightening up the house. Then she went and talked to her neighbor, Opal, and asked if she would let Shadow out of the house a couple times to go to the bathroom while she was gone. Opal, of course, had no problem with taking care of Shadow. She had watched him a couple times before and loved to be with him. Jenna knew that Shadow would be spoiled by Opal and gave her a key to the house before she went back home to get ready to go with Keith.

Finally, Jenna heard Keith drive up and her heart beat fast just from knowing she would be next to him soon. She opened the front door to her house and saw Keith walking up the sidewalk wearing jean shorts and a t-shirt along with a baseball cap. She could feel her pulse quicken as he got closer and she couldn't stop smiling at him. She knew she was falling for him and the feelings of desire and panic conflicted with each other. But knowing that there was no excuse to call the day off now, she grabbed her bag, said goodbye to Shadow, and headed out the door.

Sometime later, as they arrived at the Complex, Jenna felt a different kind of excitement and hurried out of the vehicle. Even though they had arrived two hours before the game would start, the parking lot was completely filled. There were thousands of fans tailgating and standing in front of the gates ready to get in. The atmosphere was loud and enthusiastic and after what seemed only minutes, the gates opened and they filed into the complex to find their seats.

Jenna sat down next to Keith and soaked in all the sounds and smells of the game. She could hear vendors yelling their queries to sell peanuts and colas. She could smell the warm peanuts and the aroma of beer in the air. Jenna pulled her hat down to shade her eyes and looked into a sky with no clouds to be seen and was happy she had put on sunblock. It was a humid day and her shirt was already sticking to her back and when a soft breeze wafted across the fans, she could hear people moan with pleasure from the welcome coolness. But when she heard the crack of a ball being hit and felt her chair vibrate with the roar of the crowd, she forgot all about the heat.

The following hours were immersed with hollers, screams and a few boos from the pack of people. She watched as a fly ball flew into the stands and fans tackled each other as they tried to claim the memento. She laughed at the sight of the team mascot as he danced on top the dugout and blew kisses to the crowd. He would jump up and down when the team scored a home run. All the while, she felt Keith beside her, enthralled in the game with yells at the umpires and screams to run faster.

When the last ball fell from the air and the teams disappeared below, Jenna and Keith began the long wait to get back out of the complex. When she walked through the gate leading to the front of the complex, she took a deep breath and was pleased to have freedom of movement again. She had felt like a sardine in a can and had been restrained with the thousands of people surrounding her.

Dizzy from all of the excitement, Jenna took a seat on a bench and Keith sat beside her. He gazed into her eyes and for a moment she thought he was going to kiss her. She felt warmer than she had already been and closed her eyes anticipating his lips on hers. But instead of a kiss he pushed her hair behind her ear and stroked her cheek with the back of his hand. Disappointed she opened her eyes and sighed. “So, now what do you want to do?”

“I really don’t know. This day has been incredible. The fans for a baseball game are just as loud as for a football game. I was impressed.”

“I really liked it too. But right now I really need to find a bathroom and something to drink.”

Keith laughed. "I have to admit I didn't think you would be able to sit that long without going to the bathroom." He pointed ahead of them. "I bet that shop has one and something for us to drink. Let's head that way."

Jenna walked beside Keith into a building where they were making fudge. After returning from the bathroom she joined Keith and watched the staff behind the counter. Instead of just making fudge, these people made it into a show. There was singing and dancing while they swirled sections of the fudge into the air with a long spatula. The workers would work the fudge until it was formed into a log and then samples would be given to the growing crowd watching them. Jenna and Keith enjoyed a sample before they moved back outside and headed towards the waterfront.

Looking around, they both admired the old ships docked along the edge of the harbor for visitors to see and explore and decided to do some exploring of their own. So, the next hours were spent visiting an aquarium and an art museum. After getting their fill of the attractions, they sat with a soda, on some concrete steps, and watched as performers sang for money to be thrown into a hat. As Jenna took in the atmosphere, she enjoyed the contrast of the old buildings in the distance mixed in with new structures made of glass and steel but mostly she enjoyed Keith sitting beside her.

Jenna looked at Keith and smiled. "So what do you think? Is this the best time ever or what? I, personally, have had a ball. I'm not even close to tired."

"It has been, yet another, adventure with you. It's totally different than yesterday. That's for sure. Yesterday was quiet and peaceful and today is well ... loud."

"That's okay though right?" Jenna got a knot in her stomach and wondered if this had all been a bad idea.

"I was just noticing the difference. I didn't say I wasn't having a good time. It's just yesterday I could get so close to you and feel you and kiss your warm lips." He paused. "Yesterday was a day that I'll never forget. You looked good in your bikini and felt so good in my arms. I kind of wanted our next date to be the same." He looked at Jenna and saw her begin to frown. "Now, don't get me wrong, I'm having a blast, I just wanted to be closer to you."

Jenna giggled. "You're close to me right now. I know we're not alone but we're still close. I'm finding out that I like to be close to you and it scares me, a lot."

"Don't start getting those old feelings and close me out. I still want to know so much about you and I'm determined to keep you with me." Keith nudged Jenna on her leg. "You know I mean I want to be with you in a healthy, nonviolent way, right? I hope you are figuring that out. I'm me and no one else. I'm not hiding anything or trying to get you backed into a corner."

Jenna was amazed how well Keith guessed her past. "I know. I know you are a good egg, but sometimes it's hard for me to drown out the voices in my head telling me to run, to get out. I don't know if they'll ever go away." Jenna shook her head and tried to concentrate on what was happening around her. She watched a man break dance on a piece of card board and couldn't imagine herself doing anything so dangerous. He was taking so many risks spinning on his head and landing on his back with a thump.

Keith touched Jenna's face. "Jenna, look at me please." He waited until he had her attention. "Hey, look. I know your past was rough. I'm not going to tell you it wasn't. I don't know all the details, but I can tell. But you need to realize it is just that, the past. You need to learn from it and move on. You're letting it hold you hostage. You're letting it smother out your heart until you are going to forget how to love and let go all together. Now, I'm not a psychiatrist but I've had things happen to me too."

Jenna looked at Keith with confusion and anger. She could not believe he was telling her to let go. If it was that easy she would have done it years ago. No one understood what she was feeling but her. He had known her for a short time and was already trying to analyze her and tell her what she needed to do. How dare him. She pointed her finger at him. "Really? You have had *things* happen to you? Have you ever had to … " She put her head down and looked at her shoes. She wasn't going to tell him her story. She wasn't going to cry in public.

"Hey, I didn't mean to … I shouldn't have said anything. I'm sorry. I don't know how we got onto this subject anyways. Sorry if I was the one to bring it up. I wasn't trying to do that. I just … I just wanted to let you know … Oh forget it. I don't know what I'm saying. Forgive me, please?"

Jenna wanted to forget the whole conversation. She didn't want the day spoiled and she was sure Keith didn't either. She took a deep breath and looked up at him. "It's okay. You're not the first one to try and dissect my life and try to fix it for me. No big deal. I'll figure it out and you probably are right on some of the stuff. Anyways, let's go for some dinner. We're going have to head home pretty soon. It's a long drive back and you have to start work this week. Don't you?"

Keith sighed. "Yes I do and thank you. Let's go get some grub."

They strolled towards a café, hand in hand, and Jenna admired the sun reflecting off the glass buildings, creating colored light. She looked around at everything and fell in love with the sounds and smells of it all. She looked at Keith and thought he might feel the same way. He was looking around with a smile and his eyes were sparkling with the setting sun in front of them. She liked that they walked without talking and the previous conversation was already put into the past. She held his hand and enjoyed his fingers intertwined with hers. It made everything okay to have him near her and she was content having him by her side for the day. She exhaled and smiled.

# chapter 9

THE NEXT WEEK seemed endless for Jenna since Keith had started working long hours at his new job. When she spoke to him, he sounded exhausted as he tried to lead his new group while also learning the way the company functioned. They talked a few minutes every evening, but it never seemed like it was enough.

Keith had come into her life like a whirlwind and now it was only a small draft. She was surprised how she had allowed herself to like this guy and how she was not afraid to start a relationship with him. He was changing her mind about relationships and it seemed natural to be with him. She would never admit it, but she missed him.

She tried to get back to her normal routine and occupied her time with a couple of smaller photo shoots and worked on pictures. Although, she found that her favorite thing to do was to look at the pictures that she had taken while at the island with the ponies. She studied the ponies, birds, and landscape and when she really concentrated on the pictures, she could feel Keith's lips on hers, if even for a brief moment. Just thinking about his kisses made her tingle and she missed him even more.

Jenna sat back in her chair and let her mind take her back. She enjoyed the nice memories while they were at the island. She had felt so free from her past and had managed to get a few good pictures of Keith too. But her favorite photo of all of them was when he smiled at the camera when she had asked him to look mean. His eyes seemed to dance in the picture and she longed to see his hazel eyes up close, face to face.

Jenna sighed and pushed back from the computer before she stretched her aching back. She needed to get away from the pictures and her work.

Grabbing Shadow's leash, she decided to go for a walk around the neighborhood. She loved to smell the ocean air and watch Shadow sniff the ground for a rodent to chase. He would walk with his nose to the ground and would not look up until he knew they were home. His tail would wag like a fan and his excitement would build as he picked up on a scent of prey. Shadow never caught anything, but he never gave up on the quest and Jenna thought she could learn from that. To never give up on what you want.

Summer was in full force and the evenings had gotten warmer. The breeze from the ocean didn't feel as cool and Jenna's tank top started to stick to her skin. She wiped sweat from her forehead and knew it was time to head home. She decided it was time to have a drink in the backyard and just the thought of sitting with a cold refreshment in her hand quickened her step towards her house.

She knew she was almost there she saw the tall Black Locust tree on the corner next to the Henrys' new gazebo. As she rounded the corner she noticed a shadow of a person knocking on her front door. Instantly, she felt the hairs stand up on the back of her neck and wondered who would be visiting so late in the evening. Glancing around, she looked towards the street and saw the familiar SUV. She got heart palpitations and she almost dragged Shadow, from her pace, to get home.

Keith began to head back to his SUV after he had knocked on the door with no reply. Slowly walking down the sidewalk, he heard his name. He turned towards the voice. "Hey there. I was trying to surprise you but I'm the one who got surprised. It is *so* good to see you."

Shadow greeted Keith with his tail wagging as he ran in circles. Keith patted the top of Shadow's head. "Guess he remembers me."

"Yeah," Jenna started to say as she stepped closer to Keith. "I thought it was weird he liked you the first time we met. He is usually more timid around men. Especially tall men like you." Jenna breathed in Keith's cologne and winked before giving a flashy smile. "I guess he can sense a good guy when he sees one."

"Now that's quite the compliment and I'll take it. Thank you."

Jenna placed her hands on her hips. "I wasn't expecting to see you at all this week."

Keith raised one eyebrow and took a small step back. "You want me to go? I can. I'll be sad and lonely but I can go if that is what you want."

Jenna smiled. "Get over here, mister," she demanded. She pulled his waist towards hers and gave him a hug, again, breathing in his aroma. She let the smells of his cologne, soap, and aftershave; all blended together, fill her nostrils with a perfect breath of masculinity.

Just as fast, she pulled away to look at him from top to bottom. He was wearing a dark blue suit with a black-and-blue striped tie loosened around the neck of his white shirt. When she looked at his face, his eyes looked tired. She overlooked the tiredness and speculated it was from the new job. "You look pretty good all cleaned up. I never thought that I would date a guy who wears a suit every day of the week."

Keith threw up his hands. "Hold on. You thought we were dating?" he asked jokingly.

Jenna hugged herself and looked down towards the ground. "Oh, I guess I meant ... " She could feel perspiration on her back and her mouth went dry. She felt used and knew she should never have let her guard down. He did not feel like she did.

Keith said, "Jenna, you need to learn to relax. I'm teasing you. I already said that I was going to take you on a lot more dates. I would consider that as dating." He put his hands to his sides and let out a loud sigh. "Please, look at me and don't think I'm going to run away." He gently put his hand under her chin when she didn't respond and lifted her head so that she would have to look at him. "Now show me those green eyes."

Jenna looked at Keith but felt shy and confused.

He gave a soft smile. "Now that's better." He paused for a second and kissed her on the cheek. He held her hands in his and looked at her with seriousness. "Now, on to a different topic, do you have something cool to drink? I'm pretty darn warm under this suit. I didn't have time to change because there was somewhere I really wanted to get to."

Jenna looked at Keith's large hands and felt secure with her hands in his. She knew she needed to loosen up and quit taking everything he, or anyone, said so literally. But she didn't know how. She felt embarrassed and uneasy about the situation and did not know what to do or say to make it better. Looking at the ground she kicked at some grass growing between the cement of the sidewalk, trying to buy some time to think.

Keith looked down at Shadow and saw him panting hard from the heat of the day. "Shadow, it looks like you're thirsty too," he said and paused to see if Jenna was looking at him. "Now you have two guys who need something cool for their thirst."

Keith got down on his knees and lifted Shadow so he was standing on his two back feet. Keith put his face by Shadow's and put out his bottom lip and Shadow panted beside him, staring at Jenna.

Jenna couldn't help but smile watching a large man, in a suit, on his knees with a little white dog, trying to look sad. "Okay, okay, you win. Let's go inside," she giggled as she walked to the front door. She left Keith outside with Shadow so that he could bring him inside also.

Keith entered the house and looked around. "Wow, this isn't too bad, Jenna. I can almost hear the ocean just sitting in your living room." He looked down at the coffee table. "Are any of these shells from the ones we found?"

Jenna grabbed two beers from the fridge and saw Shadow drinking from his water dish. She opened the bottles and walked back to the living room. "No, I put that together a few years ago. How's the new job going anyways?"

Keith took a beer from her and walked around the small space of the house, looking around as if trying to figure out who she was. He took a big drink and then wiped his bottom lip. "It's going fine. I'm starting to figure out how they run things. I think I'm beginning to get through to some of the older employees. They're having trouble taking direction from a younger boss. I totally understand them but, on the same note, I haven't done anything for them to not respect me. So I get upset that they don't. Overall I guess I could say that it is going okay. I think that I'm going to like it after I figure it all out." Keith spun slowly in a small circle looking around. "By the way, I like your house. It's very, what's the word, engaging."

Jenna watched as he looked around and he peered through windows and doors. He wandered into the kitchen and then looked back at her computer desk. He took a drink of his cold beer and slowly moved to the desk. He fumbled through some of the pictures and glanced at each one. There were pictures of wildlife, landscapes, people of all ages, and pictures of him at the sandcastle competition. Keith looked through the photographs of him and let out a breath. He held out a couple of the pictures for Jenna to see. "Were you spying on me or stalking me?" he asked.

Jenna ran a hand through her hair and took a big drink of her beer. She knew she should've put those pictures somewhere else. She needed to think fast. "No, no, no." She tried to sound bored. "You got it all wrong. I had a contract to take pictures at the sand castle competition. I can show you the paperwork if you want," she said pointing to a file cabinet by the computer desk. "I had been there all day and then later, I went to John and Kathy's diner. That's the same day you came along and Kathy offered you a drink and some shade to cool down," she added to refresh his memory. "Anyway, when I got home and started to go through the pictures I noticed you in a few of them. I simply wanted to see how well the picture quality was, so I focused on a subject in the back ground which just happened to be you." She took a deep breath and a large swallow of beer. "So I printed a few off to, let's say, study the quality and I guess I forgot to throw them out. See, it's as simple as that. That's all." Jenna leaned against the wall and watched for his reaction.

Keith went over to the couch and sat down. "Hmm. So let me get this straight. You took pictures at the competition but didn't realize I was in them. Then you met me right after that at the diner, then just happened to see my face in the photos later? So you focused my face up close to see how good of a picture you took?" He crossed his arms and studied Jenna's face. "If you think I'm cute all you have to do is say it. You don't have to take pictures of me when I don't even know it," Keith said. He smiled at her as if trying not to laugh.

Jenna took another drink just as Keith finished speaking. The silliness of it made her laugh, and sprayed her beer all over Keith and her couch. "I'm so sorry."

Keith stood up with the unexpected shower and looked at her in bewilderment. They both started to laugh and Jenna ran to the kitchen to grab a towel to wipe up the mess.

Keith dabbed what he could off his suit and shook his head. "Jenna, you're definitely, by far, the most confusing, amazing, mysterious, fascinating woman I've ever met. I'm anxious to see what happens next." He grabbed her hand in his and then reluctantly started to walk to the front door. "With that I really do need to get going. I wanted to see those green eyes since I don't have a hundred pictures of you, but I see you can look at me anytime you want. I have a bunch of work to do yet tonight but I'll have the weekend free. Any ideas what I can do?" he asked with raised eyebrows.

"Well, I have the weekend free also so … "

"Then it's a date." He clapped his hands once, as if to finalize the agreement.

Jenna jumped when he clapped but then remembered the pictures Keith had taken of her. "I do have a picture of myself that you took, if you want it. You didn't even cut my head off."

Keith stepped towards the computer desk like a boy getting a new fire truck for Christmas. "Of course, where's it at?" He started to shuffle through the pictures.

Jenna pushed his hand away, grabbed the picture from the bottom of the pile, and handed it to him. It was a picture of her dancing on the sand. She had on her bikini but she hadn't felt ashamed at all about her body. She thought she looked pretty good and printed the picture off for herself to have for future years when her body didn't look so young.

Keith looked at the picture. "Whoa! Now that's a keeper. You could be on a calendar or a Sports Illustrated magazine. You look more natural and more beautiful than some of those other ladies do. It's not even airbrushed."

Jenna felt herself blush. "Just don't show anyone. Okay?"

"No way." He held the picture to his chest. "This is all mine."

Jenna smiled at him and was happy that he liked the picture. She felt a twinge; she wasn't ready for him to go. "I know you have to go, but do you really have to go?"

Keith sighed. "Jenna, there's the confusing part of you. Yes, I really got to go or I'll be working all day tomorrow." He paused and rubbed his chin as if in deep thought. "Now what is it that I'm forgetting? Oh yeah," Keith said and then he pulled her to him and kissed her passionately.

Jenna's knees went weak. Instantaneously, she wrapped her arms around his neck so she wouldn't fall and also so he couldn't get away. She tasted his tongue and kissed him with equal passion. Warmth formed between them, hotter than the summer heat, and it got hotter by the second. She hadn't felt these emotions in years and was not about to let them get away.

Jenna pulled Keith tighter and could feel the heat build under his suit. She wanted him even closer and to be connected in sweet desire. Her mind was numb and she could not think of anything but the hunger between them.

"Jenna … I … " Keith tried to speak.

"No, not yet," she moaned in return.

Keith softly pushed against her shoulders to separate their bodies. "I'm sorry. I really need to go. I need to go so I can spend the day with you tomorrow. Please."

He looked into her eyes and she could see the hunger in his and was unsure why he stopped. She put her hands at her sides to prevent herself from wrapping them around him again. Her lips felt numb and warm at the same time, and her eyes felt heavy like she had become intoxicated. She looked down, opened the door, and motioned for him to leave, afraid to look into his eyes again or to even speak.

Keith took a deep breath. "I'll see you tomorrow, sweet Jenna." He touched her cheek and walked out only to turn his head slightly back to the door. "Thank you for the picture and have sweet dreams."

Jenna closed the door behind him and slid down to the floor. She started to cry, not because she was sad, just the opposite. She felt happier than she had ever felt in years and she was fearful of what would come next but knew she was willing to find out.

# chapter 10

JENNA LOUNGED IN her bed and didn't want to get up. She curled up with Shadow and rubbed his belly enjoying the laziness of the morning. She was about to fall back asleep when the phone rang. "Hello?"

"Hey there Jenna. Sorry I'm calling so early but I missed you. I wanted to get the day started right away. Hope that's all right with you?"

Jenna heard Keith's voice and felt her heart beating hard in her chest. Her breathing grew heavier. "Yeah, that's okay. I guess let me shower and get some coffee then I should be good to go. Do you have any idea what you want to do?"

"I was thinking the old fashioned way of dinner and a movie. Well, in our case, breakfast, maybe lunch, and then an early movie."

She laid back on her pillow and stretched. "Breakfast, maybe lunch, and a movie?" she said in a tone which was teasing suggesting he was expecting a lot from her. "I accept! Give me at least an hour."

"Just call when you're about ready and I'll be on my way." He paused. "Oh yeah, do you know where a theatre is and what time they would start?"

Jenna started to laugh. "Yes, I do. I even know where to have breakfast if you don't."

"Give me a break. I'm the new guy in town, remember?"

"Oh, I guess I forgot. Now hang up, mister, so I can get my coffee so I'm not cranky later," she said, chuckling, and hung up the phone.

Jenna knew the day was going to be wonderful because she wanted it to be. She was not going to let her emotions affect the day and she wasn't going to worry about the future. She had to accept that she did not know if the relationship would turn out badly and had to stop thinking like it would. She didn't want to ruin the relationship before it had even started. The idea was to have a positive attitude towards the new association and not let her past ruin it.

She looked at Shadow still lying on the bed. She felt bad not spending time with him but he didn't seem to mind or know the difference. All she had to do was give him a rawhide bone and he was content for hours.

After a while, Keith drove up and she got into his SUV for the first time. She gave a nod of approval and noticed he kept it clean with the smell of his cologne lingering. When she looked over at him she saw he was wearing gray colored shorts and a button down shirt. He glanced at her, gave her a small kiss on the cheek and held her hand as they drove to the restaurant. They went to a pancake house, not too far from Jenna's house, and sat down and filled their bellies with French toast, bacon, and eggs.

Jenna watched Keith enjoy his breakfast and felt it was nice to be with him. His sense of humor was welcoming and he made her smile, sometimes until her cheeks ached. He touched her face as much as he could and ran his fingers across her lips. He seemed to love to touch her, just little gestures, but it made her feel special and wanted. He opened every door for her and held her hand at every opportunity. She felt comfortable with him but the usual tug from her past began to seep into her mind and scare her more and more, even after she tried to push it away. The feeling rose in her stomach and she didn't want to be trapped or end up in another bad situation. It began to be more than she could manage and she had to feel safe.

"Keith? Does your vehicle run good?"

"Yes, as far as I know. I didn't have any troubles getting here from Iowa. Why?"

"What would you do if it broke down? Would you want me to let you use mine?"

Keith furrowed his forehead and set down his fork. "What? No. I'd rent a car until mine got fixed. What's with the questions, Jenna?"

She sat back in her chair. "I'm just trying to figure you out. No one is who they seem to be."

"So you're not who I think you are? I'm really confused right now."

Jenna felt tears starting to well up in her eyes and felt foolish for letting her emotions affect her like this. "I just don't want you to take advantage of me in any way. I'm trying to protect myself."

"Okay. We need to talk." Keith grabbed some cash from his wallet and laid it with the meal ticket. He stood behind his chair and looked at her with sincerity. "A pancake house isn't the best place, so would you please go on a walk with me?"

She got up and walked out the front door with him right behind her. He grasped her arm and swung her around and gave her a tight hug. Then he took her hand and pulled on it gently to get her to walk with him.

They began to walk on a bike trail that was right next to the restaurant and started to go towards a little park that was not too far from them.

Keith took a deep breath. "Okay. Now, tell me what's going on with you. Have I done something? I understand women can be a little moody but this is different."

"What are you saying? That I'm a freak? That I'm weird?" she said, pulling her hand from his and hugged herself.

He stopped, held both of her arms and looked directly into her eyes. "No, I'm saying there is some dark secret. We can never totally be together if you don't tell me what it is."

She closed her eyes. "I'm scared. I'm afraid you'll see me as weak or stupid and won't want to be with me anymore. That's why I came here five years ago. That's why I don't date. That's why … " She started to cry. She couldn't help it. She was confused and she didn't want Keith to look at her differently. She felt like she had ruined everything that they could have had.

"Hey, hey, hey," he said, softly stroking her hair. "There are only a few things you could do to drive me away, and I'm sure you are not a vampire or a secret agent. That's just a couple of the criteria I have."

Jenna giggled softly and felt dumb for crying. She wiped her eyes and took a deep breath. "Okay. I'll tell you." She took another breath and blew it out before she spoke. "There was a guy, Neil. I thought I had fallen in love with him. I did everything and anything to try and make him happy. I guess that is how I thought love was back then. I didn't know any different. Like, not long after we had started dating, he told me the cops watched for his car. He lived in a small town and he was afraid of being pulled over because his license was suspended. I don't know why it was but I didn't care either. I was in love with him and that was all that mattered. I was sure it wasn't his fault and it was the cops picking on him. But then he needed to get his car back to his place after being detailed. He asked me to drive it and he would drive my car. I questioned him but he told me that if a woman was driving that they wouldn't stop me. I didn't want him mad at me or to cause a problem so I agreed. And sure enough, I got pulled over for expired tags and received a ticket. When I got back to the house and told him, he just laughed. I told him he should pay the ticket since I did him a favor and it was his car and he laughed harder. He said it wasn't his fault I got the ticket because I was the one driving. And you know what? I paid the ticket. I believed it was my fault it happened. It was then that I started to question myself. It was something small but had a huge effect on who I was. It was always small things that he influenced me on, but they always had a big impact in the end. It was little things like that, that seemed to eat away at my subconscious. It appears so small and irrelevant but it became something so much bigger." Jenna watched their shadows stretching in front of them and tried to get control of her emotions before she continued. "I lost track of who I was and became what he wanted. But I never did the right things and it never was enough to make it so we would go a day without arguing. But somehow he had a hold of me emotionally and psychologically. I still don't know how he did it but within a few months he distanced me from all my family and friends, *or I should say I allowed him.* He had a way of saying things that always made me wrong and him right. I became a marionette on a string and tried to please him so he would want me. But in the end, there was nothing I could do to make him happy. I could tell you a thousand different stories of what he did but that would take hours. It still amazes me how I can tell what he was doing now but I didn't see it at all then." She paused momentarily and watched two butterflies dance with each other in a cluster of flowers next to the road. Just by seeing their beauty and remembering how they became that way she felt stronger for a brief moment. "When I'd get to the point of leaving he'd fill my head with promises of things he was going to do for me and I would eat it up and stay with him. I wanted to believe that we were a good couple and that I was good enough for him to want to have. I wanted to believe that I was helping him become an honest and loyal man. Then when I felt we had a chance again, he would start to stay out every night with his friends and other women. He would treat me like I didn't matter. Like I was garbage. Disposable." She felt her heart ache with regret. "Then when my family tried to intervene, I took his side because I was totally hypnotized by him. That was the worst thing I did. It ruined my relationship with my family and I lost all ties with all my old friends. Finally, one night, I got the courage to leave. I provoked him while he was drunk and ... " She raised her hand to her head and felt the crease in her skull where it had cracked. "Now I have a reminder of him on my head for the rest of my life. He had thrown me into a door and cracked my skull. When I got away from him I pressed charges and got a restraining order but I don't know if it was enough. And now I don't know if I can trust another man. I'm sorry if it frustrates you because it frustrates me too. I want to trust again, I just don't know how." She looked at Keith and felt defenseless. "I'm learning again who I am and will not use what happened to me as an excuse to become a lesser person than I know I can be. I'm slowly regaining my relationship with my family, but it's going to take a while. I said some pretty horrible things to them and they're all as bullheaded as me. Besides that, I don't know the right way to say sorry to them. I guess that's it."

She stopped walking and stood in one place, not knowing what to expect. She looked at the ground and didn't want to look at Keith, not knowing how he would be looking at her. She expected him to walk away. But then she felt his hand on her face and he raised her head so she would have to look him in the eyes.

"Okay, my turn." He put one finger up in front of him. "First, that guy is pure scum. To mentally and physically abuse you means he is a coward. I would like to know who he is and take care of him right now. But one day he will be judged and my hand would mean nothing compared to what he's gonna get." He put another finger up. "Secondly, you're the strongest woman I've ever met. To go through what you did and not use it as an excuse? That in itself is commendable. But becoming the woman you are today is truly wonderful." He took her hand and gave it a small kiss. "You still have so much love in you, which you show in the pictures you take. So you need to know that he did not break you. You won!" Keith said. "You need to tell yourself that you won." Keith held on to Jenna's shoulders and looked into her eyes. "I don't think you are weak or stupid. I see you as loving and trusting and he took advantage of that. He tried to suck all of the goodness out of you, like a parasite or tick, but he failed." Keith put his hand under her chin, "Hold your head up and be who you are. I want you to be who you are, not someone I want you to be. What fun is that? I'll say that you're a bit odd but I think that I am too. So, I guess, that is something we have in common." Keith touched the back of Jenna's head tenderly. "I'd heard a saying from a wise old man years ago. I never understood what he had meant until just now. He said that scars can become beautiful if you grow into them and remember the obstacle you overcame. I think he was right and that you are growing into your own."

He took her hand and they turned around to start to walk back towards the restaurant. They walked in silence for a few steps until Keith stopped and turned toward hers again. "Now, on a different note, can I drive your car sometime? It's hot!"

Jenna punched him softly on the shoulder and started to laugh. She breathed in the summer air and relished the idea of someone making her feel loved.

"Now that's the Jenna I've grown to know and like to see. I like you happy because it makes me happy. Especially when I'm the one who makes you happy," he said, nudging her on the shoulder as they continued to walk.

Jenna squeezed Keith's hand. "I'm actually glad that I told you. It feels good to let it out." She squeezed his hand again. "It means a lot that you're still standing beside me."

"There's nowhere else I would want to be. I love being beside you. I would find any way to be with you that I can. I think I'm addicted to you. I can't seem to get enough. It must be the perfume you are wearing."

# chapter 11

JENNA FELT RELAXED as they headed to shop around before the movie. Minutes later they were on the boardwalk looking at t-shirts and swimsuits before they came across an old time picture shop. People could be robbers or bartenders or any character they wanted to portray. When they took the picture it would look antique. She had walked by this shop countless times and, after a little coaxing, she got Keith to go inside with her to take a photo.

After looking at numerous pieces of clothing they decided to portray a wanted thief with his beautiful partner in crime. Keith had a tough look on his face in his western garb, holding a whiskey bottle in one hand and a shotgun in the other while Jenna held a large hand fan and had a little gun in a garter belt on her thigh. Jenna felt silly with the fish net stockings, purple boa, blue dress, and big yellow hat but when the picture came out it was a sepia color and they both looked fantastic.

Jenna observed Keith's expression in the picture and thought it was adorable. "Oh, you sure look tough, yet cuddly."

"I must say, you look pretty hot in those fish net stockings," he said and shook his hands like they were on fire.

"Yeah, yeah. Here's a picture and frame for you too. Now you have two pictures of me." Jenna said as she handed Keith his copy of the picture.

Keith spoke in his best John Wayne voice. "Why, thank you, little lady."

Jenna shook her head at Keith then looked at her watch to see they had thirty minutes until the movie started. "Would you mind going for a drink at John and Kathy's?"

He pretended to tip a hat. "Well, madam, I'd be obliged."

"Okay, we're out of the store. You can quit talking like that at any time," Jenna said as she giggled.

"I think I would fit in fine in the Old West. Don't you think so?"

"Yes, you would."

When they reached the diner, Jenna practically ran to her favorite table before another couple sat down.

Walking up to the table, Keith chuckled. "What is it with you and this table?"

Jenna shrugged and sat down. "I don't know. I guess it's the first table I sat at and it has a nice view of the beach."

Just as she ended her sentence, Kathy came out with two lemonades. "It's so good to see you. And you're together." Kathy clapped her hands and had a huge smile as she looked at Keith and then at Jenna. "I was starting to worry about you. I didn't know if he had whisked you away and married you or what happened. I knew he was a sweet boy when I first met him, but I didn't know if you'd figured it out yet."

Jenna rolled her eyes. "Yes, yes, I figured it out. And no, there's no wedding ring," she said as she displayed her empty left hand.

"Keith," Kathy said as she looked in his direction. "You are a godsend. This girl needed someone like you in her life and it's about time." She grabbed his hands and held them momentarily in hers.

Keith grinned. "Well, I actually needed someone like her in my life too. I was missing something and now I know what it was. It's only been a short time since we really started dating each other, but I can't wait until the day I can say that we have been together for a month or a year." He said looking over at Jenna.

Jenna put up her hands. She was surprised by his comment. "Whoa there, mister, let's not get ahead of ourselves. One day at a time, please. I need time to adjust." She paused. "And trust."

Kathy stood in front of them and watched as Keith and Jenna spoke to each other. She puffed her chest like a proud momma bird and hollered into the doorway of the diner. "John. John get out here!"

Within seconds, John stepped into the sunlight and put his hands by his eyes to shade them. "What's so important? I have burgers to tend to." He looked under the umbrella and saw Jenna and Keith as they sat casually in their seats. He looked at Jenna and squeezed her shoulder with his hand. "Well, I'll be. Don't you two look good together. I was just telling the Mrs. the other day to not worry about you. I said that you'd make the right choice when you had to choose. Looks to me like you made the right choice with this man sitting next to you." He winked at Jenna and patted Keith on the back as he looked at him. "Keith, I'm sure you have figured out that she's like a daughter to us and we expect her to be well taken care of or you'll have Mr. Addams to answer to," John uttered in his gruff voice. He headed back to the door of the diner to tend to his burgers.

Keith called out to John as he walked away. "Yes sir I will."

Jenna looked down at her watch, took a big gulp of her lemonade, and stood up. "Well, we need to go to catch a movie." She looked at Kathy. "I promise I'll stop by in the next couple days."

Kathy gave each of them a quick hug. "Well. That was too quick of a visit. You better stop by soon, I miss talking to you."

Jenna gave Kathy another hug. "I wanted to stop so you knew I was all right and I miss talking to you too." Jenna blew Kathy a kiss as they walked away and watched as she headed over to the other tables to talk to customers.

Keith took Jenna's hand in his and playfully swung their hands in the air as they walked. He looked over at her and wiped his forehead with his free hand. "Whew! I didn't know I was gonna get threatened by a giant. I consider myself big but John made *me* feel like a midget."

Jenna smirked and liked the idea of John trying to protect her. It made her feel loved. "He really is a big teddy bear although I think he meant it."

Keith agreed. "Yeah, I think he did."

# chapter 12

As Jenna and Keith walked through the crowd of people at the carnival, the smells brought Jenna's thoughts to when she was a child and had gone to the fair with her family. She had perched on top of her dad's shoulders, while looking out at all the people, and had felt safe. Her dad would hold onto her knees, so she wouldn't fall, as Jenna ate cotton candy up above him. She missed those days and ached to talk to her family and ask for forgiveness. But knowing that wasn't going to happen today, Jenna directed her attention back to her surroundings.

Between the music and sounds from the rides turning and tilting, carnival workers calling out to people to play their games, and screams from children being tipped and spun on the rides, it was hard to focus. But through it all Jenna could feel Keith holding her hand in his and he squeezed it softly as they weaved through the mob of people. They walked through the crowd until they ended up in front of a Ferris wheel.

Keith looked up at the tall ride turning in a circle with people secured in the separate cars. "I don't know about this. I don't tell too many people, but I'm afraid of heights."

"Oh." Jenna grabbed his arm and felt his muscles under the t-shirt. "I never would have guessed that, with you being such a muscular guy." She looked at him with honesty. "It's good to know that even someone like you has a weakness. We don't have to go. I don't want you uncomfortable."

"Well my biggest weakness is actually you." he said and fluttered his eyes at her.

"Why mister … ?" She paused and put her hands on her hips. "Okay. What's your last name?"

"Tell me yours first, Miss Jenna … ?"

"Roberts. That's my last name … Roberts. And yours is … ?"

"Well, missy, my name is Keith Christensen." He gave a little bow towards her. "Nice to meet you."

"This is our fifth date and just figuring out last names. We're taking this way too slow."

"Well, technically this is our sixth."

Jenna tilted her head to the side. "Sixth? How can it be our sixth?"

"I considered changing your tire to be a short and unexpected date also."

"Changing my tire a date?" She frowned. "Since you brought it up, why were you there when I got a flat tire?"

"That's a secret." He put his finger to his lips. "Shh."

"No, seriously, why were you there, Mr. Christensen?

He looked up and sighed. "I'll tell you when we're on the wheel of fear. It's our turn."

Within seconds, they stepped up and sat down in the car connected to the large wheel. A man secured the bar to hold them inside then pushed a lever to make the car move up into the air. Keith's hand tightened on Jenna's as the car began move back and forth and tightened more as they ascended into the air.

Jenna grimaced from Keith's hold. "Relax. Please. Relax or you're going to break my hand. We didn't have to go on this thing."

Keith relaxed his grip a little. "I'm sorry. I wanted to break my fear of heights but I don't think it's going to work out like I had planned. I guess this wasn't such a good idea."

"Just look at me and try to calm down. Tell me the story when you showed up and changed my tire. I'm really curious about that. I thought it was weird the day it happened. Was it fate or coincidence?"

"I think it was a little of both," Keith started. "Would you believe that I was lost? I was trying to get to know my way around and ended up on that road. I was trying to find my way back to my place."

"You weren't even close to town when you stopped to help me."

"I know. I saw a car on the side of the road and thought I could stop to help and maybe get some directions in return. I was going the other direction so I had to do a U-turn and pulled up behind you. And then ... " he paused, "And then I saw the most beautiful woman turn from her car wearing a skirt. I knew it was you from the diner and I couldn't believe my luck."

Jenna liked the compliment and remained as still as she could to keep the Ferris wheel car from moving. "You never asked me for directions."

"Of course not. I didn't want to look like a fool in front of you."

Jenna looked at Keith, and couldn't believe how they were on the same road, at the same time, and she had gotten a flat tire right then. It had to be fate. Then she felt the Ferris wheel start to go in a continuous circle and saw Keith's jaw clench.

The ride began to slow down and their seats were at the top of the Ferris wheel. Jenna looked around and saw other people rocking their car to make it lean back and forth as hard as they could. Other people were looking down at the ground, below them, laughing and smiling. But when she looked over at Keith, she could see he was losing the color in his face and sweat beads forming on his forehead. She felt sorry for him and wondered why he even agreed to come on the ride if he was afraid of heights. It was a side of him she had never seen and thought it was kind of cute; although she was glad the ride was almost over. She didn't want him to get sick.

Jenna squeezed his hand to get his attention. "Hey, look into my eyes and try not to think about where we are. You're fine. I'm so sorry I suggested coming on this thing. What do you want to do after we get back to the ground? Is there anywhere you wanted to go?"

Jenna saw Keith get pale and was happy when the Ferris wheel began to descend back to the ground. As the wheel lowered and the man raised the bar for them to exit, Keith could not touch his feet to the ground fast enough. Jenna noticed that the man controlling the Ferris wheel had a smirk on his face when he opened their car and saw Keith's fear. She gave the man a dirty look and took Keith's hand to lead him away.

"That was embarrassing," Keith said. He wiped the sweat from his forehead and looked like he was trying not to throw up.

Jenna took his hand and led him to a nearby bench. "A Ferris wheel is definitely crossed off the list of things to in the future. Don't worry about it, I won't tell anyone. It's our secret."

"I'd appreciate that. I have some dignity I want to hold on to. But thanks for helping me out up there. I'm scared to think how it would have gone if I didn't have your hand to hold."

Jenna secretly felt remarkable. For the first time she was the hero instead of the victim. It was nice to help someone out and be acknowledged for it. "How about a water or soda?"

"Good idea. I want to get as far away from this thing as I can right now."

As they walked away from the amusement park, Jenna and Keith strolled down the boardwalk and enjoyed the scenery and each other's company. Keith's nausea was finally gone as they sat down on a bench to eat funnel cakes. They watched as the sun began to set next to the water.

Jenna thought the colors were magnificent. The sky had swirls of blues that turned to purple and yellow that turned to red. The way the colors moved in the sky seemed to match the movement of the water and she had to look hard to see where the sky ended and the water began.

The gleam from the sun, which was reflecting on the water, seemed to turn to sparkles. These sparkles were then carried by the waves up to the shore. It was there that they were turned into foam to be left on the sand. The sand drank in the water and left seashells poking out of it like little treasures left behind for all to see. Children ran to pick up the shells and then ran from the waves squealing with delight. The waves crashed on the shore and the water looked as if it was trying to reach out and touch the children before receding back to the ocean.

Jenna was pulled from her trance as Keith slapped his knees with his hands and stood up to stretch his back. He looked at her and reached for her hand. He smiled. "Should we head home? It is starting to get late and I'm sure that your pup needs to get outside."

Jenna sighed. "Yeah, you're right. We better get going."

They headed towards the parking lot as they held hands. Jenna leaned on Keith's shoulder as they walked. They didn't say a word, but Jenna still felt comfortable and didn't want the night to end.

As they came around a corner of a building, a group of men were walking from the opposite direction. The men had obviously been drinking and as they passed, one of the men bumped Keith on the shoulder. Then he turned around and pushed Keith from behind.

"Are you messing with me?!" the man yelled at Keith.

The other men stopped and smiled as their friend pushed Keith a second time. Another skinny man chimed in. "Yeah, I think he's messing with you. What are you going to do about it?"

Jenna saw Keith look at the five men in front of him and then he looked at her with a mixture of anger and dread in his eyes.

The man pushed Keith a third time and spoke in a demeaning voice. "What? Are you scared to look bad in front of your little girl friend?" He asked and then looked at Jenna studying her curves.

The man's eyes had hatred in them and Jenna could tell he was not going to back down. She felt Keith's hand grasp hers tightly. He tugged on it and they took a step back.

The man stepped towards them matching their step backwards. "Oh, the little boy is scared. He probably even hits like a girl. Maybe I should have his woman fight for him?"

Keith had a stern expression and looked at the man and pointed down the boardwalk. "Okay, that's enough. Be on your way."

"There you go; it looks like I hit a sore spot. You must have it bad for this chick. She sure is pretty. Maybe she wants to come with us and have some fun. We could show her a good time. I'm sure we'd make it more fun than you ever could."

The man's friends started to laugh and Jenna watched as they made obscene gestures towards her. Her whole body went stiff and nauseous with fear. She looked around to see if there was anyone close who might be able to help them, but she saw no one. She could hear voices and music from a night club but no one was walking in their direction.

Keith stepped in front of her so she was out of the men's view. "Man, you're way out of line and need to back off."

The man gestured to his friends and they started to turn to leave. "Okay, we'll go. Just having a little fun, that's all."

Keith took Jenna's hand again and they stood still and waited for the men to start walking before they would turn their backs to them.

"Oh, one more thing." the man said with his back turned to them. As quick as lightning he turned and hit Keith right in the face.

Jenna watched as Keith fell to his knees and the man started to laugh. After a couple seconds the man became silent and turned his attention to her.

He raised his fist. Jenna closed her eyes and waited for him to hit her but heard him grunt instead.

The man snorted. "Let's get out of here. These two are a drag."

Jenna couldn't believe it had all happened so fast and Keith was still on his knees. She watched as the men walked down the boardwalk patting each other on the back. When the men were a good distance away Jenna got down on her knees and looked at Keith. "Are you all right? Please let me see. Do we need to go to a hospital? Can you stand up?"

She was frantic. Keith had his hand to his face and blood was dripping through his knuckles. There was no way for her to tell where he was bleeding from or how bad. Jenna cursed under her breath for not having some tissue and she looked up and saw a portable toilet. Standing up she ran to it, took the whole roll of paper from it, and ran back to Keith. Quickly unraveling the tissue, she unrolled a handful of the paper and handed to him.

He put it under his nose and stood up. "Sorry Jenna," he said and sounded congested.

"You have nothing to be sorry for. Those jerks did it. You didn't do anything to them. Do you need to go to the hospital?"

He seemed to be fighting back tears. "No, I think I'm okay."

"Do you mind if I drive your truck? My place is closer and we need to stop the bleeding and get some ice on your nose," she said and was not going to take no for an answer. She put her hand out for the keys.

He sighed and acted defeated. "Fine."

So after arriving at the house and stopping the bleeding, Jenna got Keith an ice bag to help with the swelling. She plopped down on the couch beside him and Shadow jumped on her lap. "Keith, I'm so sorry all of this happened. I wish there was a way I could've prevented it. I'm also including the Ferris wheel in the apology."

"Unless you forced me on the ride at gunpoint and set up the guy to punch me, you don't have any reason to say sorry. It's not your fault. I'm just sorry I didn't hit him back. The only reason I didn't is there was five against two."

Jenna raised her eyebrows. "Two?"

Keith moved the ice to a different position. "Oh yeah, I bet you would have gotten a punch or two in."

Jenna put her hands in front of her like a boxer. "You think I'm that tough?"

"Yes, I think you could be if you needed to. But I guess my main reason is this. Have you heard the phrase I'm a lover not a fighter?"

"Why yes I have. Are you saying that you're not a big tough guy?"

"I am when I need to be, but I'm mainly a lover."

"A lover, huh?" Jenna felt a growing desire and didn't know if she could control it for very long. Even with his nose swollen, she was extremely attracted to Keith. She wanted to know how his mouth tasted and his skin would feel next to hers. "I'll be the judge of that."

Keith took the ice bag from his nose and tried to smile without his eyes watering. "Hmm, that sounds interesting. How do you plan on proving that to me?"

She had Shadow get off the couch and got up on her knees. She leaned towards Keith and bent over to give him a kiss. "Well, I suppose I can start like this."

Keith leaned his head so he could kiss her without hurting his nose and let out a groan of frustration when he could not. Jenna felt a growing urgency to be touched and ignored the groan before she proceeded to kiss him on his face and neck. She was desperate to taste his mouth, but knew it was not possible for the time being and would have to improvise.

Within moments of caressing each other, Jenna felt his desire in the way he held her tightly, wanting to be close too. Feeling his urges gave her even more of a hunger for him. She felt a need that had to be satisfied and knew Keith was the man to take care of it.

Keith's arms tightened around her and she could feel the warmth beneath his shirt. She knew the chemistry between them was growing and she wanted to reach the boiling point. There was such a repressed desire within her and she felt a growing wakefulness being next to him. Surrendering to all of these emotions, she let them take control. She straddled Keith's lap, so they could be even closer. He let out a moan, which made her want him even more. His skin got hotter against her lips and she could feel he was ready and willing to satisfy her needs.

They touched and grabbed and pulled as they tried to fulfill their needs. She knew she wanted more and this was not quenching her craving. She pulled back, looked into Keith's eager eyes, and smiled. She took his hand and led him to her bedroom, where no man had ever entered.

They dropped down onto the bed holding each other. A new appetite came over her and she nearly ripped his shirt while removing it. His pants fell to the floor while his hands were on her, finding skin to touch and caress. Most of her clothes were removed without her even noticing. She could only feel the heat being emitted from his hands and finger tips. The movements and sighs had her in a state she had never been. She wanted to taste his flesh and feel him within her. She wanted to be gentle and rough at the same time.

The temperature between them made the room feel like a sauna and his touch made her reach an emotion beyond words. His fingers, legs, and hands touched her flesh and left a trail of goose bumps after them. Jenna wanted to scream and cry and laugh all in the same moment. She felt like she had no control over him or herself. But behind the moans and gasps, she thought she could hear a continuous ringing in the background. Wanting to have Keith even closer and needing him closer, she could not pull herself from the ecstasies of his sensual body to hear it clearly. As she went to clench him and pull him to her, there was a familiar voice in the distance. Recognizing the voice, Jenna was quickly brought back to the view of her room.

Jenna heard Kathy's voice in the kitchen and it sounded frantic on the answering machine. She heard the words, scared, hospital, John, and heart attack. She was up before Keith could react and was picking up the phone.

# chapter 13

JENNA SAT IN the visitors' area of the hospital and fumbled through the pages of a magazine. She heard the doors to the front of the hospital open as she threw the magazine onto a table. Glancing up, she saw Keith and took in a breath when she saw his swollen nose. But even though he looked miserable, she had to hide the excitement she felt from him walking through the door.

Her heart began to beat faster and she could not believe that he had taken the time to come here. She felt a sensation she had never felt and was proud to have him there with her. She smiled at him but then she remembered where she was and why she was there and her smile faded.

Jenna grabbed his hand as he sat down. "We don't know anything yet. The only thing we know is that John had a heart attack. We don't know how severe, but he is stabilized right now." She reached out and touched his cheek and looked at his nose again. "Are you okay?"

"Don't worry about me right now. I'm fine." He said calmly.

Jenna watched as he stood up to go sit next to Kathy. He took one of her hands in his and lightly squeezed. "Hey, how are you holding up? Can I get you anything? Some coffee or tea?"

Kathy looked up at him and her eyes were swollen from crying. She wrung the tissue in her hands and tried to force a smile. "Thank you, but I don't need anything. I'm glad you came here for us. A strong man is good to have around right now."

Keith sighed and squeezed her hand again. "Well, from what I saw of John, he looked pretty strong too. A strong man will come out of this stronger. Okay?"

She patted Keith on his knee before she looked back down at the floor. "I hope so, dear. I hope so."

As Keith sat back down next to Jenna, a doctor came into the visiting area. He strode over to Kathy and began to discuss the situation. He informed them that John was stable but he would have to stay a few days for observation and possible surgery. The hospital had a lot of tests they wanted to perform and wanted to monitor him closely for the next couple days. Kathy gave the doctor a hug and followed him back towards the ICU.

Jenna watched Kathy and doctor disappear through a door and her heart ached for John and she hoped everything would be alright. She couldn't imagine being with someone for as long as Kathy and John had and then having him torn away suddenly. But in the same breath, she hoped she would have someone to be with for that long and share so many memories together. She felt Keith sitting beside her and wondered how long they would be together. She looked at him and felt her heart skip a beat thinking about a long relationship with such a nice guy. "Keith, I really appreciate you being here but you don't have to stay."

"I'm fine. I want to be here for you and Kathy." Keith looked around the empty room with a puzzled expression. "Is there anyone else coming here tonight?"

"No, they don't have any children and they were both the only child in their families."

"The way they are with you. I assumed they had kids. They seem so loving to you."

"They are. They're like my parents while I'm away from my other parents." Jenna took Keith's hand in hers and was happy she could have a connection with him. The hospital felt so cold and having Keith sit next to her seemed to warm her from the inside to the outside. "Kathy had complications when she was younger and isn't able to have children of her own. She had been in a car crash a long time ago not long after her and John had been married. It was after the accident that they had found out she had been pregnant and she had lost the baby. Then she had to have an emergency hysterectomy, due to some bleeding from the accident. Even now she says she can feel the emptiness where her womb should be." Jenna looked at the ceiling and then back down to Keith's hand in hers. "It had to be a hard time for Kathy to not know the child she had growing inside of her. I've never experienced it but I don't ever want to either." Jenna took a deep breath and couldn't imagine how Kathy had felt. She touched her stomach and wondered if she would ever experience pregnancy and how it would feel. She shook her head and focused on what she was saying. "But then, years later she and John tried to fill the void by taking in foster children. Kathy told me the kids they raised turned out wonderful and grew to be accomplished adults. They were proud of the children they had helped. They still have a lot of pictures of them displayed in their house. When Kathy looks at them, I can see the pride in her eyes. She cherished them all." Jenna felt tears welling in her eyes. She was proud of Kathy and John and how big of a hearts they had for other people. She felt Keith squeeze her hand and squeezed his hand in return. She continued. "They have so much to give. I'm so happy to have them in my life. But, to sum it up, they fostered a few kids when they were able to. They tried to keep in touch but they went their separate ways after time. So I guess you and I are it."

"Wow. That's sad. They seem to be such good people and would have been good parents to their own children too. That's awesome that they could give so much love to some children that needed it. Now I see why you admire them so much." Keith paused before speaking again. "Hey, what about the diner? Does it need to get closed?"

"No. Thank goodness. This happened when they were getting ready to head home. Then Kathy rushed him here and … " She felt more tears start to swell and tried to choke them back. "Kathy must have been so scared. She said that John was getting into the truck and they were talking about where to get the crab for the next day. Then John grabbed his chest, fell onto the seat and was in a lot of pain. Kathy said that she had to push him over to the passenger side and drove here. She is stronger than me, mentally I mean. I don't think I could have done that. I would have been too scared."

Keith gave Jenna a hug. "I'm sorry, but I think you would have done fine in the situation. You did a wonderful job with me when I hurt my nose. When something happens I think the adrenaline helps and if you care about the person."

Jenna liked the feel of his arms around her but she knew it wasn't fair to him. "I'm probably going to be here for quite a while. Really, you don't have to stay. I know you have to work in the morning and you need to get ice on your nose. It's really swollen," She touched his cheek and took a deep breath. "I'm sorry. I rushed out on you and left you in my house. I'm sure you didn't know how to get here either. I'm really sorry."

"No, please, don't be. I understand. I'd rather snuggle in bed with you right now, but that's the breaks of the game."

Jenna thought about how she left. She didn't even give him a chance to go to the hospital with her or even get dressed. He was still lying in the bed when she told him she had to leave. She didn't even look at him as she got dressed and rushed out the door yelling behind her what hospital. She started to tear up again. "Man. I just left you laying there. I'm so sorry. You are new in town and don't know where anything is. I left you in my house alone after we were … I feel so bad. I just had to get here and I didn't think about it."

Keith wrapped his arms around her. "Hey, it's okay. I understand. Really, I do. I gave Shadow a biscuit and I locked the door behind me. Do you need me to go back and let the dog out or … " He winked at Jenna. "Wait for you?"

She smiled. He made her feel good even under these circumstances. "No, please go home and get some rest. I'll call you tomorrow and let you know what's going on."

"I feel bad leaving you here alone."

"You really are a sweet guy, but I'm going to go see John pretty soon. You can stay if you want but I don't want you to feel like you have to. It's sweet that you even came here at all. I think it's more important for you to get a bag of ice on your nose and relax."

"Jenna, really I'm fine." Keith stood up and kicked at the leg of a chair. "If anything, I'm more worried about how the people at work will react. I've tried so hard to gain their confidence. I'm scared that the older men will look at me like I'm reckless or a loose cannon. I know they'll draw their own conclusions from how I look without asking me how it happened. I just don't want them to start to think that I'm not qualified for my job because, well, I am. So please stop worrying about me and concentrate on John."

Jenna stood beside Keith and hugged him. He hugged her back and she felt safe in his arms. She closed her eyes and enjoyed the moment and wished she could feel this way all the time. "All right, I'll quit but I'm going to go his room and be there for a while."

Keith pulled her away and looked into her eyes. "Alright, I'll go, but I expect a phone call in the morning. Just remember that I'm worried too. Take care of yourself." He paused for a moment. "Hey could you tell me something though? I really don't know where I am and need directions to get back to my apartment."

# chapter 14

WHEN JENNA OPENED her eyes, after drifting asleep between nurses yelling and ambulances making noise outside, she noticed there were a few more people in the waiting room with her. She wondered when they had come into the room and looked down at her watch to see it was three thirty in the morning. She had dozed off for an hour and hadn't heard a sound.

Jenna rubbed her face with her hand and noticed she was still holding a cup of coffee in the other one. She was amazed the cold cup she was holding had not spilled while she slept. She shook her head, stood up to stretch her aching muscles, and walked to the bathroom to dump the cold drink down the drain. When she looked up from the sink she glanced into the mirror and saw her eyes looked tired and puffy. She put some cold water on her face, to try and wake up better, and tried to stretch her muscles a little before she went back into the waiting area.

She felt like a zombie as she wandered back to the waiting room and poured a fresh cup of coffee hoping it would help her be more alert. For a moment, she watched the steam rise above the cup and felt the heat come through it. The steam seemed to put her in a temporary trance as it rose from the cup and she had to shake her head to bring herself back to reality. Jenna took a drink of the hot liquid and then slowly walked down the hall to check on John and Kathy.

When she stepped into the doorway, the soft rhythmic sound of the monitor beeped with John's heartbeat and a television played quietly on a dresser. The room had white walls and the bed had white linen. The equipment for John's heart and the bed frame were an off white color and it all made the room feel cold and disconnected. Jenna took a drink of her coffee to feel the warmth as a shiver ran down her spine.

She looked over to John. There was a tangle of wires connected to sticky pads on his skin and tubes lying across the bed and his body. He looked pale and weaker than she had ever seen. His face looked like it aged from the last time she had seen him and he looked frail. He was sleeping soundly and she almost started to cry as she looked at him and thought about if he would not be in her life anymore. He meant a lot to her, as did Kathy, and she had grown to love them both.

As Jenna turned and admired Kathy she noticed that her hair had fallen from the bobby pins holding it, and it was cascading down her back. Jenna had never seen her hair down like this in all the time she had known her. She couldn't tell if Kathy looked older or younger with her hair like it was, but she looked different. She looked softer and more vulnerable as she was asleep in a chair next to John's bed and had her hand on John's and her head rested on the bed.

Watching Kathy sleep, Jenna reflected back when they had first met. She had been so reserved and Kathy had taken the time to try and talk to her and make her feel comfortable. It had taken a few visits before she started to open up to Kathy and shortly after that they were good friends. They began to tell each other stories of their lives and that is when Jenna had learned about the car accident. Jenna had confided in Kathy about Neil and Kathy had taken Jenna's hand in hers and told her what a strong woman she was to get away from such an awful man. It was then that Jenna began to see Kathy as a mother figure and treasured every moment they had spent together. Then later, when Jenna had met John, she was amazed how such a large man could be so gentle. It had given her a small amount of hope that there was a man like that out there waiting for her.

Jenna smiled at them and couldn't move. She seemed to be stuck in the doorway entrance watching John and Kathy sleep. Her thoughts drifted to her own parents. She did not want something like this to happen to them and not feel the same as she did when she stood next to John and Kathy. They were her parents and it was because of her that their relationship had been hurt. It was time to heal the wounds that she had caused. She hadn't talked to them for two weeks now, and hadn't mentioned Keith at all. Her and her family should have a better relationship by now but every time she talked to any of her family it felt strained. Her mom always offered and invitation home but Jenna turned it down every time she asked. Maybe it was her that made the talks tense and it was not as bad as what she made it to be.

Frustrated with herself and the situation, she sat down in a chair, next to the wall, and gave herself a hug. She felt comfortable to be in the room with John and Kathy and her eyes got heavier every second she was with them. Her thoughts traveled to Keith for a moment but the heaviness of her eyes won and they closed.

After what seemed to be only a few seconds, Jenna was startled as a nurse came in to check John's vitals. The nurse seemed sweet and was gentle while she worked with John. She tried hard not to wake him but as she took his blood pressure his eyelids started to flutter open.

Jenna watched as John slowly started to wake and blinked at the light in the room. He opened his eyes and looked around. Jenna wanted to rush to his side but she knew that it was Kathy's time with him and she remained quiet as they interacted.

She saw Kathy wake up as John moved his hand and she grasped it and kissed it repeatedly. "You're all right. Thank God you're all right." Kathy said.

John whispered. "What happened? I don't remember. Why am I here? My throat is burning. My ribs hurt."

"Sweetie, you had a ... a heart attack." Kathy paused and cleared her throat. She wiped the tears from her face and smiled at him. "I'm so happy that I can see your beautiful eyes looking at me."

John's eyes would close and he would open them just as fast. "How?"

Kathy rubbed his hand and patted it. "They're thinking it could be high blood pressure. They're going to do more tests to find out but ... " She took a breath. "But you might have to have heart surgery."

Jenna stood up as she saw John's eyes close and his hand slipped from Kathy's. Jenna was scared.

Kathy looked panicked. "John? John? Are you okay?"

The nurse looked over at John and then at Kathy, from the machine she was inspecting next to the bed. "He's fine. His body has a lot of healing to do and he has a large amount of medication in him. He's going to sleep quite a bit for now." She began to walk towards the door to leave and stopped before turning back to Kathy. "You should try and get some rest too."

Jenna felt her heart ache as she watched Kathy's tears fall onto her cheeks. As Kathy wiped them away, she watched John sleep. Quietly she rose from her chair and glanced in Jenna's direction and saw her look back with tears running down her face too.

Jenna wiped her face and threw her arms around Kathy and squeezed her tight. "I'm so sorry all of this is happening. You two are such good people and it's not fair that you have to experience the pain you are going through. I love you both and I … " Jenna started to cry again. She had tried hard not to, but she couldn't stop the tears. "I don't want anything to happen to either of you."

Kathy patted her on the back. "Oh sweetie, I'm so happy that you're in our life and here for us right now. We can never determine what will happen, but to have good people around makes it easier. Whatever comes our way will be a simpler trial to get through having each other to lean on," she said and then put her arm around Jenna's waist. They held each other tight as they walked out of the room.

Kathy stopped outside the door and leaned back on the wall. "I can't pretend to be strong anymore. I'm trying to hold onto the fact that John is a resilient man, in body and soul. I need him to be okay. It's hard to do when he is lying in that bed like he is." She put her hands up to her head and started to weep. "Oh, Jenna, what am I going to do if something happens to him? I can't bear the thought of him being gone. I have nothing without him and I don't know how I would survive if he wasn't in my life. I don't think I could live without him. I don't think I'm that strong." She put her hands over her face and couldn't speak.

# chapter 15

JENNA'S BODY WAS exhausted and her movements felt robotic. Over the last few days, she had tried to go between the hospital, her home, Keith, and work. Now she was the paying the price, feeling sluggish and tired.

Her life felt like it was on a merry go round and someone had pushed it to see how fast it would go. All the energy had been sucked out of her and everything she knew had been pulled out from under her. Jenna fell back on her pillow and Shadow laid by her side. She wanted to try and regain her composure but as she tried to relax, her thoughts always went back to John.

She couldn't believe how strong he was and she wished she had some of his inner strength. He had gone through multiple tests for his heart already and didn't complain during one of them. He'd had an electrocardiogram, numerous blood tests, a nuclear heart test, and an exercise stress test. His doctors were astounded by him and said he was an impressive patient.

When the final tests came back, they concluded that it was, in fact, high blood pressure. When they read the results Kathy had tapped her feet on the floor, like a dancer, and had raised her hands in the air singing hallelujah. Jenna and John had both laughed. They were all happy that John would not have to undergo surgery but he would have to change how he lived.

After a couple more days, Kathy had begun to act like herself and had a sparkle back in her eyes. She appeared to cope better with the situation and it was planned for John to go home within the next couple days. It could have turned out so much worse and Jenna was happy for them both and glad that John was still in her life.

Jenna had tried to visit as much as she could, but there was not enough time in the day to do everything. In just a few days she had begun to neglect her home, work, and Keith.

But she was mostly worried about Keith. The last few times she had spoken to him, it was strained and he seemed distant. He was always pleasant on the phone, but he sounded distracted and uninterested in talking to her.

Jenna had not seen him since the night she rushed to the hospital, and wondered if she should go see him. She'd never seen his apartment before, and thought about just dropping by, but she wondered how he would feel if she showed up, unexpected. She was interrupted by the phone ringing in the kitchen.

"Hello?"

"Hi. Is this Jenna?" a male voice asked.

"Yes, it is. Who's this?"

"How sad. You don't recognize my voice Jenna? After all we had shared together."

Jenna felt her skin get clammy and the hairs stood up on the back of her neck. "Neil?" she asked in a quiet voice. She prayed the answer would not be yes.

He spoke in a condescending tone. "Why, yes it is. Boy, it took a long time to track you down. You're still not close to the family, I found out. Why'd you move so far away from home, Jenna?"

Her body went tense, her stomach started to tighten and her mouth went dry. She leaned against the kitchen counter to hold herself up. "How'd you get this number? Never mind, I don't care! Don't call me again. I want you to leave me alone! Leave me alone!" she shouted into the phone and fought the urge to throw up.

"Ah … Jenna come on. You know we go together like peanut butter and jelly. I want you back. So what do you think? Want to have dinner tomorrow? The beach is sure pretty. I hope … "

Jenna banged the phone back onto the cradle. Neil's voice had sounded so close, and when she heard it she felt like she was back in Idaho again. She looked at the phone with repulsion and disconnected the cord from the wall. Looking around the room, Jenna felt sick with fear and ran to the windows and doors and made sure they were locked tight.

Shadow was startled by her quick movements and whimpered, lowering his head with a look of bewilderment in his eyes. Jenna tried to soothe him by scratching his ears, but it was tough to calm him down when she could not calm herself. She looked down at her hands and they were shaking uncontrollably. Struggling to control herself and figure out what to do, Jenna went to her bedroom with Shadow and barricaded the door shut.

She sat down on her bed and felt numb. She couldn't handle any more emotional drama. Tears streamed down her face as she collapsed onto the bed. She rubbed her temples and tried to relieve the headache that was forming behind her eyes. Tears continued to slide down her cheeks and she couldn't stop thinking of how Neil found her. Why did he find her? How did he know she was at a vulnerable time in her life again? Should she call the police? Should she move?

Jenna slammed her fist into her pillow. She was mad and scared and confused. She slammed her fist a second and third time. She continued until her arm was tired and no more tears were falling.

Jenna put her head back on the pillow and tried to think. But no matter what, she didn't understand how Neil had gone to jail for what he did and now he wanted her back into his life? How was he not deterred by the jail time and restraining order? How did he find her again? Why did he find her again? What did he want from her? Jenna banged her hand against her head and tried to think of who knew she was even living here. Neil had already ruined her relationships with all her past friends. Her family, even if they were not on good speaking terms yet, would not tell him. Did he con the post office? Her head was spinning with questions. She felt like she was drowning and there was nothing to grab onto to help her get above water.

Shadow jumped up beside Jenna. He stretched out next to her oblivious to the situation and looked at her face. He licked her arm and closed his eyes as he cuddled up next to her. Jenna curled up and hugged her legs with one hand and stroked Shadow's back with the other. She felt calmed by his presence and she rocked herself back in forth until she could not think or keep her eyes open.

As she woke back up, Jenna felt sunshine warm her face through the openings between the shades in her room. Taking a deep breath, she stretched and smiled but suddenly the thought of last night's phone call invaded her thoughts. She clenched her fists and felt the sting of her nails digging into her own palms. A scream rose in her throat and her stomach started to curdle. She ran to the bathroom and threw up until there was nothing left.

Jenna flushed the toilet and slowly pushed herself up from the floor. She dragged her feet as she went to brush her teeth and tried not to gag on the toothbrush when it touched her tongue. Then she had to muster up any strength she had left to open the bedroom door and dragged her feet towards the kitchen. She felt defeated by the world.

Shadow was happy as ever and was unaware to her state of mind and wagged his tail, ready for his morning treat. Jenna knew he would need to go outside to relieve himself and she felt a twinge of fear when she thought of Neil being out there. She was nervous to let him go out, afraid what might be on the other side of the door. Momentarily, she thought of putting some newspaper on the floor for him but knew he would look at her confused. He was too well trained.

Jenna hit her fist on the counter from frustration. There was no way she was going to live in fear. She was not going to let Neil take control of her life again. Reminding herself of the tattoo on her back she tried to recall why she got it and knew she needed to change her life to live stronger and happier.

The butterfly was to represent her rebirth as a stronger woman and she was not going to lose sight of that because of a phone call. Taking a deep breath, she opened the door for Shadow, but then couldn't help scanning the yard to see if there was anyone around. Jenna shook her head from disappointment in herself and closed the door.

Just as she did this, she heard a knock on the front door. Her eyes darted around the room to look for a place to hide. But then, just as quickly, she found some inner strength and crept to the window to peek out. Her heart was beating fast and her hands felt clammy as she pulled the window curtain back to see who it was. She took a deep breath when she peeked from behind the curtain. She saw a man was already walking away and she exhaled.

It had only been the parcel delivery man. He was an older man who came to her house at least twice a week with contracts or other items for her business. Usually she would say hello or wave to him but not today. She grabbed the package from the steps and closed it just as fast.

Jenna put the package on her coffee table and opened it slowly and cautiously. She sighed with relief when she saw it was the new keyboard she had ordered for her computer a few days prior. She giggled to herself and felt silly, and put the box on the couch to take care of later.

"Okay, enough is enough." She said. She needed to clear her head and couldn't handle any more of the drama. She needed a break.

Looking through her emails on her computer, Jenna found a contract for a battle reenactment in Pennsylvania she had read a couple days earlier. Scanning the email she knew they had put out the contract late and if she bid now she would have an answer within a couple of days. They needed someone soon and she hoped it would be her. Frantically, she filled out the necessary paperwork and faxed it as soon as she was done.

Just as the fax machine beeped and displayed that the fax had been sent, she heard her cell phone ring in the kitchen. Jenna jumped when she heard it and her mouth went instantly dry. Hesitating, she looked at the caller id and saw it was Kathy.

"Hello?"

"Hi, sweetie, it's Kathy. Just letting you know we are heading home tomorrow for sure. John just got the okay from the doctor. Are you all right? You sound, well, scared."

Jenna sighed with relief and sat down. "Oh, that's wonderful news. I'm sure you and John are both ready for that." Jenna paused. "And don't worry, I'm fine."

"Okay, I won't worry about you then. But after being in this place, all I can say is this certainly is not any kind of home and honestly, I can't stand the smell. But John is back to his usual self. He is worried about the diner and I have to keep telling him its fine. He's a stubborn man sometimes. The diner is the farthest thing from my mind right now." Kathy spoke with excitement and seemed more at ease. She sounded well rested and ready to take on the world.

Jenna envied her and didn't want to ruin her enthusiasm by saying anything about Neil and decided to keep it to herself for the time being. "Hey, I do have some news of my own. I might have a contract for a battle reenactment in Pennsylvania. I'd leave in a couple days and be gone for a few days after that. Are you all right if I go?"

"Jenna. Sweet Jenna. You do what you have to do. I know you worry about us, but try not to. We'll be just fine. Have you told Keith?"

"Well," Jenna said slowly. "He's been acting kind of ... I don't know. Kind of distracted, I guess you could say. I don't think he would care if I went or not."

"Of course he would," Kathy said in a scolding tone. "He's crazy about you. Things have been tough lately. Maybe he doesn't know where he fits in? You need to talk to him or you'll never know."

"I know. There's just ... " she paused. "There's more to it but I don't want to talk about it right now."

Kathy sounded worried. "What's wrong? I knew something was wrong."

"Nothing. Nothing. It's fine. I guess I'm just a little stressed. Anyway, you need to worry about John. I can handle everything on my end. Besides that, I'm happy for you both. I'll call you tomorrow to check in and let you know if I'm going to Pennsylvania or not."

"Well, since we are heading home tomorrow I was wondering if you could give me a hand around the house. Laundry and everything else has taken over and I need help. Could you help me out with some of it?"

Jenna liked the thought of getting out of her own house. She didn't feel safe here and welcomed the excuse to leave for a while. "Of course I can. I'll head over right away. Do you need anything?"

"Nope I've got that all under control and I even picked up Shadow a raw-hide bone. Make sure to bring him. But best of all I got us a nice bottle of wine that we can sip on as we clean. That sounds like a nice combination doesn't it. Cleaning and wine."

Jenna giggled. "Yes it does. We'll see you in a few minutes."

Jenna hung up and felt bad. She didn't like to hide information from Kathy. But Kathy had enough on her plate right now and Jenna didn't want to add more.

# chapter 16

KATHY THREW HER towel on the counter when she heard Jenna and Shadow walk in the door. "Hi there sweetie. Thank you for coming to help me out because I don't want to be cleaning all day. I want to get back with John as soon as possible. He picks on the nurses if I'm not around to watch him."

Jenna smiled as she walked into the kitchen and forgot about Neil and Keith when she smelled fresh baked banana bread. "You spoil me so much. I love it."

Kathy winked at Jenna and gave Shadow his rawhide bone. Then she handed Jenna a slice of warm bread and they both sat down at the kitchen table.

Jenna had a couple bites of the bread and then looked at Kathy. "How do you do it?"

Kathy looked at Jenna with a look of satisfaction. "Well, I guess it's because I add an extra banana to the recipe. I think it gives it just a little bit more flavor to make it delicious. I'm glad you like it."

Jenna giggled. "No not the bread, even though it's awesome. I'm talking about how you are handling all the pressure with John and the diner and everything else. I don't know how you do it. I'm a wreck about my life and it drains me. You seem to keep a smile on your face, most of the time, and keep going. You're so positive."

"I guess it's because I have faith that everything happens for a reason and will work out. I try not to sweat the small stuff so I have more energy for the big things in life. Then, when things like that come up, I just try to remember that the situation won't last forever." Kathy put her hand on Jenna's. "It's also important to remember that something good always come from it. Although you may not be able to see the good right away, it does happen. Sometimes it's hard to remember, in that moment, but I try to."

Jenna listened to what Kathy said and knew she was right. She was making everything bigger than what it was. She needed to stop worrying about every little thing that happened because it was making her exhausted and crazy. She needed to let it go and handle it when it needed to be handled. There was no need to worry about what could happen. She loved the philosophies Kathy had and they always seemed to help.

They finished their bread in silence and then Kathy grabbed some wine. "Here you go. Let's have some fun cleaning."

The next hour was spent with brooms and cleaning supplies in hand. They cleaned everything from the toilets to the sinks. Jenna fell on the couch and closed her eyes. "I'm not use to so much domestic work. I need a break."

Kathy fell on the couch beside her and laughed. "Oh Jenna, you need to work those arms with a dust cloth and mop. It'll get you in shape in no time at all. How do you think I got such a beautiful figure? " Kathy patted her full figured belly and laughed until she had tears in her eyes. "I needed a good laugh."

Jenna laughed with her. "It's always good to laugh. They say that laughter is the best medicine. I need to do more of it too. I think you're good for me."

"Well of course I am. Now get off your butt. We have some windows to clean and some laundry to work on. But first we need to refill our glasses. We don't want to get thirsty while we're working so hard, do we?"

Jenna grabbed the wine from the counter and filled both their glasses to the brim. "What do you think will happen with Keith and me? I sometimes wish I could tell the future so I wouldn't get my heart broken."

"I think you and Keith will do just fine. You need to just let things go as they go. Don't try to hurry anything and don't dissect everything until you find a flaw or it will never work. Just remember that everyone has flaws and learn how to deal with them. I could tell you a lot of drawbacks with John but over time I would miss them if he stopped. Don't get me wrong, his little habits, although not unhealthy, still drive me crazy but it is part of who he is."

"You give the best advice. But sometimes it's easier said than done. I guess I need to learn how to prioritize my problems and quit making them worse than what they are." Jenna looked down at a basket of clean laundry. "Umm, I don't have to take care of John's underwear do I? That's just a little weird for me."

"Of course not." Kathy's smile became a serious expression. "Thank you for being there for me Jenna. I mean, if you hadn't come to the hospital the other night I don't know how I would have taken it. I know I just said to keep a positive attitude, but I was terrified of losing my husband and felt guilty for not seeing any warning signs. Did you see any? Never mind. I guess the main thing is that it came out good and we can correct the problem with good food and exercise." She paused. "It will be good for us anyways. We spend all day together at the diner but really don't have time to talk. I think a nice walk every now and again will help with our relationship too."

"Well see, something good came out of the situation. You just proved yourself true. And just so you know, I was happy to be there for you. I wouldn't be anywhere else, as Keith found out the hard way. I felt bad leaving him."

"Speaking of that, what were you two doing?"

Jenna blushed. "A girl never tells. Besides that, it was probably good anyways to slow us down a little. Things were heating up pretty fast."

Kathy gave a mischievous smile. "I remember those days. That was a long time ago for John and me but I still remember like it was just yesterday. I remember how you feel the electricity in the air and the temperature rises in the room. Yes, I remember those days well."

"When do I know when it's the right time? I mean, I don't want to come off as I'm desperate but I don't want him to think I'm a tease. Maybe I should wait until we reach the "I Love You" phase. I get confused on the subject. I guess I haven't had much practice in that area."

"Well, I suppose my advice on that is to do what you think is right. Don't go overboard or be unladylike with the situation, if you know what I mean. Just be natural. Don't force it."

"I think that I found a good guy, or should I say he found me? Whichever, I think we'll be okay. I just wish I could reach into my brain and take out all the bad memories so that they can't influence the memories meant to come." Jenna thought about the phone call from Neil and wondered if she should bring it up. She shook her head and decided to keep it to herself, at least for right now. "I hate what happened to me and I still feel sick when I think about what I allowed. I had grown up with such a good family and would never think I would become so weak. But I didn't even know it at the time. I thought I was being so strong to stay with him and make him happy. I thought I was being such a good person. Man, I was stupid. "

"You weren't stupid and you didn't *allow* anything. You simply trusted in the wrong man. And I do use the word man lightly, in his case." Kathy took a drink and stared at her glass. "Like I said before, I think some good comes out of everything. I guess I would have never met you if you hadn't moved here and you wouldn't have moved here otherwise. So, that's something good for me. And you know what to look for that are signs of a bad egg, don't you?"

"I don't know if I do or not. I didn't see the signs before so I'm scared I won't see them if they happen now. I guess that is what scares me the most with Keith. What if I really start to like him and he ... "

"Stop right there. First of all, you really *do* like him already. I could see that the other day. And secondly, how old am I? Don't answer that. But because of the experience from my age, when I met Keith, I don't see a bad bone in him. I think I did pretty dang good picking out John and I see a lot of the same loving characters in Keith. Remember he did come to the hospital. He came there for you. Not too many new boyfriends would do that?" Kathy took a drink and almost talked into her glass. "I know I liked it he came there."

"Yes, you're right again. How did you get this way? Did you have a past life as an *all knowing monk* or something?"

"No, I just simply listen and observe. That's the key. I tell you, I see all kinds come through the diner and I've gotten pretty good at pinpointing their personalities before they leave. Now I tell you what. We can keep talking but we need to get working too. I want to get back to the hospital and I believe you were going to go see a special someone." Kathy winks at Jenna. "Weren't you?"

"Yes I am. I was a little hesitant before, but now I'm anxious to see him. I need to let him know how I feel. Let's get busy."

# chapter 17

JENNA WATCHED AS Keith loosened his tie, got out of his SUV and slammed the door. She could hear him talking to himself. "Screw them. They don't know what they're talking about. I'm qualified for this and them not trusting me yet is bull." He kicked at the "tow zone" sign in front of his apartment building and started up the sidewalk.

"Keith?"

He seemed startled when he heard his name and turned around. Jenna was standing on the sidewalk, behind him, staring. "Hey," he said coldly. "I didn't know you even knew where I lived. Why am I graced by your presence?"

Jenna was bewildered by his reaction and tone. She met his glaring eyes. "Wow, I guess nothing. Sorry I bothered you," she said.

It felt like her heart had been stabbed with a hot knife. Her heart felt broken. She stared at him and saw such anger in his eyes and didn't know why. Just moments ago, she wanted him to hold her but now she wanted to run away from him. She had trusted him when he said he wouldn't hurt her. Jenna felt even more hurt and then began to feel angry. She was angry at Keith, but also at herself for even trying to have a relationship to start out with. Infuriated and confused, she turned and walked back towards her car.

"Really? You're just going to walk away?" He waved her off and headed back to the apartment. "Whatever, Jenna. Do what you want. You're good at that."

She felt her heart start to race and tears swell in her eyes. Turning back around, she pointed her finger at him and yelled. "What's your problem? Why are you being this way? What did I do?"

Keith turned around and pointed at himself and spoke with resentment in his voice. "What's my problem? My problem? Do you care about my problem?" He pushed his hands through his hair and took a step backwards. "No, you don't care about my problems. It's always about Jenna. It's always about how she feels and what she wants. Every phone call was all about you. Always about your stresses and worries but I had stuff to say too. I have a lot of pressures I wanted to talk about. But you didn't give me a chance. I'm tired of this relationship being one sided. It's about you and your feelings. It doesn't involve me at all. I thought I could handle it, but I guess I was wrong. I'm not a counselor." He said angrily.

Jenna took a step back like she had just been slapped in the face. She didn't know Keith could be so cold. Flabbergasted, she didn't know how to respond to him but when she thought back on it, he was right. Through their short relationship she had been insecure and needed acceptance and security from him. Then when John ended up in the hospital she had been anxious to talk to Keith about John and Kathy and her work. She hadn't given him any time to talk about his job or worries.

Looking back at him she felt a feeling of regret. She spoke softly. "You're right. I did nothing for you. I'm sorry. I was ... " She had to take a breath so she would not cry. "I was just going to let you know that I was bidding on a job in Pennsylvania and might be gone for a few days."

Keith looked caught up in his own thoughts. He spoke tenderly and with remorse. "Jenna, I didn't mean it like that."

She put her hand in the air. "No. Stop. You're right. I was too needy and you were acting as a shrink and I was depending on you too much. I know that I've been absorbed in my own problems and haven't given you the time of day. I understand." she paused. "Maybe I'll try to call you when I get back and we'll work it out."

Jenna tried to sound in control although inside she was screaming. She couldn't bear to look at him and wondered why she had even tried to have a relationship at all. It was better to just stick with Shadow. She knew Shadow would never hurt her.

Feeling crushed, she put her head down and turned and walked back to her car. With the car in reverse, she glanced back and saw Keith walking towards her. She shook her head and pressed on the accelerator. Keith caught up and was beside the car. He looked into the window and had a look of regret in his eyes. Jenna wanted to get out and hug him and to know everything would be all right, but her emotions were beyond calming down. Her world was crashing down. Keith slapped her window as she put the car in drive and sped away.

Shadow, who had been in the back seat, let out a whimper when Keith hit the window. He jumped to front seat and sat down on the passenger side. Jenna looked at him and tried to smile. "Looks like it's just you and me again, buddy. I'm no good at this relationship thing and am going to stop trying."

# chapter 18

THE AFTERNOON WAS beautiful and Jenna tried to think positive thoughts as she looked through her emails. There had no more indications that Neil knew where she was and she thought maybe he had given up. She smiled at the idea and momentarily felt free.

Focusing on her computer, she noticed she received an email from Pennsylvania and was surprised to see it so soon. After reading it she had mixed emotions of excitement and sorrow at the same time. They had accepted her bid and would need her to be in Pennsylvania on Saturday.

She looked down at Shadow. "Well, bud, looks like we're going to get out of town for a few days."

She scratched Shadow behind his ears and thought of Keith. She wanted to talk to him and try to figure out what was going on but she was too scared. She didn't want to be rejected again and didn't think she would be able to handle the pain from it either. Jenna shook her head and turned back to the computer and researched pet-friendly hotels in the area. After looking at a few, she got lucky and found a nice hotel not far from her job site.

She stared at the start date icon of when they would arrive. She sat back in her chair and rubbed her forehead, trying to think. After a few moments she decided that they would leave today. There was nothing for them here, right now, and a break sounded better and better. Maybe they could do some sightseeing and escape the drama currently haunting her.

She typed in her reservation and headed towards her room to pack. Her thoughts were focused on how many shirts to bring when she heard a knock on the front door. She was startled by the sound and laughed at herself. She walked to the door and glanced out the window.

Jenna saw a young woman standing in front of the door. She looked like she was in her early twenties and had beautiful facial features that Jenna thought would look good in her portfolio of pictures. She wore a baseball cap with long blonde hair falling against her back and her clothes hung on her like she had lost a considerable amount of weight but did not bother to buy new clothes that fit her new frame.

The young woman was holding a vase of flowers with one hand and looked down at her nails on the other. She looked up when Jenna opened the door. "Yeah, these are for you." She looked at the flowers. "They're really pretty. Wish someone would send me some flowers like this."

Jenna smiled and reached for the bouquet. "Thank you. I guess I do have a pretty nice boyfriend after all." The lady shrugged her shoulders and turned and walked away towards a van with a huge bouquet of flowers painted on its side.

Jenna closed the door and felt reassured when she looked at the flowers. Keith must have regretted the way he had talked to her. Even though she still felt hurt from how he spoke, she couldn't help but smile as she placed the flowers on the table.

Jenna opened the card that came with them, anxious to see what he wrote. She put her face next to the flowers and breathed in the delicious scent before she turned her attention to the card. The card read, "Jenna, I can't wait to see you. We have a lot to discuss. You'll be mine forever. Neil."

Jenna almost started crying and felt an urge to throw up. Her fingers seemed to burn from the card she was holding. She threw it onto the table as if it had scalded her.

Her hands began to shake and she felt perspiration under her shirt. Without thinking, she grabbed the vase and flowers and threw them into the garbage. Water from the vase sprayed back into her face and she reacted like it had been boiling hot. Grabbing a towel, she wiped the water away and then she tore the card into tiny pieces before she threw it into the garbage on top of the flowers. Then, she snatched the garbage can and held it away from her body like it had something nasty in it, scared to breathe in its scent. Finally, she put it outside the front door, slammed the door shut and locked it.

She folded her hands together to help with the shaking and couldn't believe Neil knew where she lived. He knows where I live, he knows where I live, she repeated in her mind. Jenna frantically ran to her bedroom and threw clothes into her suitcase without thinking. Within seconds she ran to the kitchen, got Shadow's food and treats, and grabbed her cell phone.

Jenna looked around cautiously as she put the luggage in the trunk and slammed it shut. Her hands were still shaking as she tried to put the keys in the ignition and she couldn't get the key to fit. After closing her eyes for a brief moment, she took a deep breath, inserted the key, and started the car. She drove towards Pennsylvania without looking back.

# chapter 19

KEITH COULD NOT concentrate on his work. He felt bad for his words and actions he had displayed last night towards Jenna. He had tossed and turned all night and only got a couple hours of sleep as a result.

Every time he closed his eyes, Jenna's hurt expression penetrated his thoughts. She looked wounded from his words. Why had she been there to start out with? He had not even taken the time to let her say why or had she? He strained to remember and could recall her saying something about a job but he could not remember anything about it. He had been to self-involved and harsh to her. That was not like him.

It had been the first time she had come to his apartment and probably the last.

He stared at his computer screen but could not concentrate on it. He played with a pencil that was in his hand, and then broke it in half with frustration. He questioned if his irritation was actually about Jenna. He *had* told her he wanted to know everything about her. That was what she had been doing.

He heard is name being spoken by his secretary. "Mr. Christensen?"

He ran his hand over his face and up through his hair and took a deep breath. "What is it Nancy?"

"Your conference call has been cancelled due to technical problems on their end. It's been rescheduled for tomorrow."

He needed that break and was going to take advantage of it. "Thanks. That's good actually. I'm not feeling too well and thought I would leave at lunch and come back tomorrow."

"Very well sir. Is there anything I can do for you or I can take messages the remainder of the day."

"Yeah, just take the messages." He grabbed his suit jacket. "I think I'm going to head out now."

"Hope you feel better and hopefully I'll see you tomorrow then," she said and hung up the line.

Keith left the office and tried to call Jenna on her phone. Her cell phone went straight to voice mail. Then when he tried the house phone it would ring with no answer of the machine and he was bothered. He had never had a time she did not answer the phone. Frustrated, he slammed his hand against the steering wheel and headed to Jenna's house. He needed to apologize and ask for her forgiveness.

Keith came around the corner of Jenna's neighborhood and did not see her car. Instead he saw a blue pickup where she had usually parked. When he looked towards the house he saw a tall, lanky man behind the bushes. The man was trying to look inside Jenna's living room windows.

"What is going on here?" Keith said out loud as he pulled up behind the pickup. He got out and walked up the sidewalk and observed the man as he moved side to side trying to see past the curtains. Keith stopped for a moment and folded his arms in front of him and studied the guy behind the shrubs.

The man looked to be in his thirties and was freshly shaven. His appearance did not give the impression that he was trying to steal something but him trying to look in the windows was unnerving. Keith didn't think he looked like a repairman but his small frame didn't make him look like a threat either.

Keith moved forward and stopped a few feet from the man. "Can I help you with something?" Keith asked with a stern tone and demanded an answer.

The man ducked down like someone had tried to swing their fist at him. He stood up and turned to see a very large man, in a suit, looking at him. "Hey. No, I'm waiting for my girlfriend and I thought I'd surprise her. You know how they love surprises," the man said nervously.

Keith felt a twinge of irritation and pointed at the man. "Your girlfriend?"

"Well, we had some … umm … troubles but I'm willing to let them go. You know chicks and the stupid stuff they do sometimes," the man said and stumbled for words.

Keith licked his top lip and tried to figure out what this man was talking about. Jenna did not seem to be the kind of lady that would have two men in her life at the same time. Jenna didn't seem to be able to hardly handle one. She never gave the impression that there was anyone else and if there was, well, she was a really good actor. "I think you have the wrong house." Keith grew angry with how this man talked about Jenna and how he remained behind the bushes like a coward. "The gal who lives here is definitely not stupid in anyway or form."

The man put his hand in the air like he was waving away a fly. "Oh sure it is." He pointed over to the flowers, shriveling in the garbage can, on the front porch. "There are the flowers I gave the bit ... I mean her." The man scrambled for the proper words.

"Well it doesn't look like she wants anything to do with you by the look of the flowers." Keith spoke sternly and motioned to the man's pickup. "I think you should be on your way."

"Oh I see how this is," the man spoke slowly and scratched his head. "You think she's yours?" He laughed. "Let me assure you that she is not and will never be. Her and I have some things to ... let's just say we have some things to discuss."

Keith grew impatient. He loosened his tie and unbuttoned the top button of his shirt. He needed to try and cool down from the heat of the day and the frustration of the man in front of him. Keith had a bad feeling. "Whose house do you think this is?"

"Well, not that it is any of your business. Jenna. Jenna Roberts. She has brown hair. Well at least it used to be brown. But anyways, she's cute and mine. Her and me go way back and I bet she'll be sure surprised to see me." He paused. "Now, I know I have the right house so back off. She's a good piece, if you get my drift, but she's mine and always will be."

Keith felt his heart pound hard in his chest. "Let me guess. Your name is Neil."

"She's been talking about me?" Neil paused and smiled. "I'm sure she turned it all around to make it sound like I'm a bad guy. She would do something like that. Anything to make people feel sorry for her." He paused again and had a smirk on his face. "I'm sure you fell for it. Don't let her fool you. She's like any other woman. You can trust them as far as you can throw them, which isn't far. Believe me, she got everything she deserved."

Keith tried to hold back his temper when he thought about what Jenna had said about Neil. He looked at him with contempt and spoke harshly. "That's enough. You'll leave now and never come back or you'll have me to deal with." He loosened his tie more and took off his jacket and dropped it on the ground. He could feel sweat run down his face and felt his hands clench into fists. Stepping forward, he watched as Neil fell over twice as he tried to move from behind the bushes.

Neil spoke with a nervous tone. "I see she got to you." He raised his hands in front of his chest, in a defensive manner, as he came around the bushes. "She has a way of getting inside your head and making you think what she wants you to. She's very convincing and will stab you in the back when she gets the chance." Neil smiled. "She's crazy man. She's psycho, if you get what I mean."

Keith shook his head. "Really? Then why would you want to be with her?"

"Well, let's just say that I know how to handle her. She's like a wild pony and has to be broken. Nothing I can't handle though." Neil raised his face in the air like he was superior. "But by the looks of it, you couldn't break her."

Keith had enough and was losing his patience fast. "All right, let's handle this like man to scum. Whoever is still standing can wait on her porch for her. How does that sound?" Keith said firmly as he took two more steps forward and Neil took a step back. Keith laughed when he saw what a coward he was. "Now I get it." Keith motioned for Neil to attack him. "Come on! If you can break a woman you can break me too. Right?" Keith took another step and felt perspiration go down his back. "Or is it you have to pick on someone that is smaller and weaker than you? Is that what makes you feel good? By having women cower down to you to help you feel macho?" Keith took another step and leaned his body forward. "Come on tough guy! Put some moves on me like you did Jenna. Make *me* fear you! Show me how tough you are!" Keith kept moving forward and was screaming in Neil's face by time he was done. "That's what I thought," Keith said and he turned away. He knew Neil would hit him when he wasn't looking and that's what he wanted. An excuse.

Just as Keith thought, when he turned his back he heard footsteps and felt a fist in his ribs. He took a deep breath and turned around. He saw fear in Neil's eyes.

Keith pulled his fist back and aimed right for Neil's face. He hit him twice without even feeling it connect. He struck Neil in the stomach countless times, until he fell onto the ground and was gasping for air. Keith had to stop the urge from kicking him until he wasn't moving anymore.

Leaning down, Keith pointed right into Neil's, now bleeding, face. "Now, you will leave Jenna alone if I'm in her life or not. You will not call, write, email, fax, Morris code, or send smoke signals. She'll think that you dropped off the face of the earth." Keith kicked Neil's lower leg. He grabbed Neil by the shirt collar and stood him up. He locked eyes with him and glared. "Is that understood?"

Neil's eyes filled with tears. "Jenna who?" he squeaked out.

Keith picked Neil off his feet for a second and then pushed him towards his pickup. "That's right. Now get your sorry ass out of here or next time I won't be so gentle."

Neil hit the side of his pickup and left a dent where his elbow struck as he fell back. He looked at Keith and then scrambled inside the pickup. He rolled down the passenger side window a small crack. "You can have her. She's used trash anyways." He quickly rolled the window back up as Keith walked towards him. Neil started the engine and squealed his tires as he drove away.

Keith watched him drive off and looked at his license plate. After he memorized the numbers on the plate he looked down at his knuckles and started to feel the throbbing pain. He walked up the sidewalk and grabbed his suit coat. He looked around to the neighbors' homes and anticipated to see people watching him from their windows. He almost expected to have a police car fly around the corner to arrest him. But as he looked around he didn't see one curtain move or one spectator watching. Keith shook his head and grinned. As he stepped into his vehicle he looked back towards Jenna's house one last time, gave a sigh of regret and drove away.

# chapter 20

THE HOTEL LOOKED comfortable and was nice for the price. Jenna looked around after checking in and found a weight room and a swimming pool with a hot tub next to it. There was also a sauna and free breakfast in the mornings. She didn't know if she would use the hospitalities but it was nice to know they were there. She and Shadow went to their room and she fell onto the bed, face down. After hours of driving she was exhausted but felt safer in Pennsylvania. No one knew she had left or where she was staying.

Shadow jumped on the bed, next to her, after he had smelled every inch of the hotel room. He rolled onto his back and showed his belly so Jenna could give his chest and belly a scratch. Jenna seemed to satisfy his need for attention and he showed his appreciation with a lick on her hand before he jumped down to smell the room again.

Jenna watched Shadow and was glad she made the decision to come here. Reaching into her purse she grabbed her cell phone and was surprised when she saw it was shut off. Her mind had been so preoccupied with the trip and drama that she'd forgotten to turn it on after charging it. Turning it on, she decided she better call Kathy and let her know she had left Maryland and got there safe.

Kathy sounded surprised. "You're already there? Well, that was sudden." She paused. "What's going on Jenna? What are you running from? Is it Keith?" she asked with concern.

Jenna took a deep breath and held back the tears that wanted to fall. "My life's so crazy right now. Keith was so cold to me and then Neil ... " she bit her tongue and wished she hadn't said his name.

"Neil? What about Neil? What did he do?" Kathy asked frantically.

Jenna started to shake and her nose began to run. "I don't know. I don't know," she whispered.

Kathy spoke with a stern voice. "What did he do?"

"He called." She paused and wiped her nose. "He called my house and then he sent flowers. He knows where I live. How do I go back to that? What do I do?"

"We'll figure it out," Kathy said soothingly. "Did you tell Keith?"

"No!" Jenna hollered, with a sound of desperation in her voice. "He didn't give me a chance. He was so distant and cold. I tried, but he said I was too demanding."

"Oh, sweetie, I'm so sorry. I'm sure he didn't mean it. He'll apologize."

"I don't think so. I shouldn't have even tried to be with him. I need to just keep to myself and forget about having anyone other than Shadow close to me. Maybe I'll get a bunch of cats too. A couple dozen of them should make people think I'm weird and keep them away. Then I won't have any problems with any relationships." She cleared her throat. She wanted to change the subject. "But enough of that. That's not why I called. I didn't even want to bring it up. How is John?"

"Don't worry about him. He's fine. He's already complaining about the diet the hospital has him on. He's kind of cranky today but he's alive and still here. That's all that matters."

Jenna swallowed back a lump in her throat. "That's wonderful. I'm really happy for you two and I'm sorry I called and brought up the commotion in my life. I really didn't mean to bring it up."

"Don't worry about us. You worry about yourself. Just enjoy the scenery a bit and take a few days to breathe. You'll figure out what to do. You're so smart and beautiful and you'll figure it out soon enough."

Jenna sighed and appreciated the idea that Kathy always knew how to make her feel better. Kathy really was like a mom to her. "Thank you," Jenna said with tears in her eyes. "You always know what to say. I'm just so confused right now and don't know which way is up or down. I thought I was letting go of the past and moving forward, but now I feel like the same scared girl I was before. I'm sorry. You need to worry about John. I guess I am demanding."

"Now stop that. Stop it right now," Kathy said firmly. "You have to talk and get things off your chest. You're as important as anyone else. You have every right to say how you feel and to have emotions. Don't lose sight of who you are. You're special and there are not too many people like you in this world. Don't become disconnected from your feelings like most of the world has done. That's what makes you who you are and makes you so special. Now, like I said, don't worry about John and me. He needs to rest and frankly, so do I."

Jenna took a deep breath. "You're right. I need to calm down a little so I can think. I do have a full day until I start working so I'll try and relax." She thought about the hospitalities of the hotel. "There is a hot tub downstairs."

"There you go. Put on a bathing suit and go and sit in the warmth. Just remember we are here for you. And if you need to, you can move in with us. We'll figure it out. Now...John is grumbling about something so I need to go. We love you, Jenna. Don't forget that. Keep your chin up."

Jenna hung up with Kathy and sat on the edge of the bed. She knew Kathy was right, once again, and she needed to unwind to be able to think straight. Without giving it a second thought, she put on her bathing suit, turned on the television for noise for Shadow, gave him a chew bone, and headed downstairs. When she entered the pool area she saw she was alone. That is just what she wanted.

The hot tub was in a massive room with windows enclosing it along with a swimming pool that went from two foot deep up to eight foot. She walked past the pool and let the smell of the chlorine fill her nostrils as she put her feet in the water of the hot tub. Liking the sensation, she slowly lowered the rest of her body down into the heat of the water. She laid her head back to let the jets under the water push against her skin and she closed her eyes. The water was hot, almost too hot, but she planned on enjoying the sensation for as long as she could tolerate it. The bubbles echoed in the oversized space of the room and seemed to drown out all her thoughts.

"Mind if I join you?"

Jenna had not heard the door open to the pool area and was startled. She splashed water as her arms covered her chest. She looked up and saw a man with jet black hair and blue swim trunks on. He had brown eyes and a cute smile. "Oh, yeah, of course," she almost whispered.

Jenna glanced over as he stepped into the water and noticed his muscular frame. She thought that he looked like he was about six feet tall and was probably in his thirties. Looking at the bubbles on top of the water, she tried to ignore him, but with all the sounds he made, it was hard to do.

He made moans like the water was burning him as he stepped in. After finally sitting down, he let out a huge sigh. He laid back and rested his arms behind his head and let out a sound of pleasure. He had his eyes closed and talked casually. "So, you here for business or pleasure?"

Jenna was startled, again, by his comment. She looked around to see if someone else had come into the room with him. Not seeing anyone, she looked back at him.

He now had one eye open and was smiling at her. "Yes, I'm talking to you. Are you here for fun or work?"

"Oh." She paused. "I guess for both?"

"Are you asking me or telling me?"

"I'm telling you."

"Well that's great. A little break is good for everyone. Staying for a few days?"

Jenna ran her hand across her face and wondered why this guy was asking her these questions. Did he know Neil? Why did he want to know so much? She felt uneasiness, but at the same time she found him interesting. She was confused.

He watched her through his one open eye. "Sorry. Don't answer that. Sometimes my mouth gets ahead of my brain." He reached his hand out for her to shake. "I'm Jared, by the way. I'm here for an old battle reenactment. I've never been in one and figured it could be fun. I don't know which side I'll be playing on, but I hope I don't get shot too soon. I'd rather run the field screaming awhile first. You ever been to a battle?"

Jenna felt at ease for a moment and thought it was funny that they were in town for the same thing, but she certainly wasn't going to tell him that. She shook his hand and looked around the room for a towel. "No, but I'm sure it's interesting. It's probably more fun than reading it in a history book."

"Yeah, that's what I think too. I've always been a "hands on" kind of person. I'd rather get my hands dirty than sip on some tea and read a book."

"Well, I like tea and a good book but I'm hands on too." She continued to scan the room and noticed the towels were on a shelf on the other side of the pool. She cursed under her breath. She was wearing a one-piece swimsuit but suddenly felt naked under the water. Rubbing her fingers together she could feel they were getting wrinkled from being in the warm water and desperately wanted to get out. Embarrassed of not having a towel she figured she would wait to see if Jared would get out first.

As she glanced back over at him, Jared had closed his eyes again. He groaned and then let out a big breath. "Man, this water feels good. I'd sleep here if I didn't think I'd turn into a shriveled prune." He opened one eye again and glanced at her sitting across the hot tub. He took a relaxed breath and sat deeper in the water. "I bet you came in here to try and relax, huh? I'll shut my mouth so you can."

Jenna looked at the shelf across the room and wished she had powers to make a towel appear next to her. "Actually I was just going to get out. It was nice meeting you, though." She stepped out of the water, grabbed her room key card, and walked quickly to get a towel from the shelf. Deciding to grab two towels, she wrapped one around her waist and another around her shoulders and chest. Quickly she turned back to the hot tub and caught Jared closing his eyes. Jenna smiled to herself and headed to the door to leave and opened it. "Good luck in your reenactment. Hope you stay alive."

"Hey, thanks, that means a lot." He paused. "Hey, I don't want to sound forward, but I'm here alone and thought maybe you would want to grab a bite to eat later?" He turned his body so he was resting his head on his hands in front of him on the edge of the hot tub. "I hate to eat alone. I feel like everyone is watching me."

Jenna turned, surprised by his forwardness, and her eyes met his. "What makes you think I'm here alone?" she asked.

He shrugged his shoulders and spoke like he was bored. "Honestly, I didn't know if you were. It doesn't matter. I'll go to eat with your husband, boyfriend, brother, or kids. I'm not picky."

"Wow, you are kind of forward, aren't you? And no, I'm not alone and I don't know if "he" would want the extra company. We planned on it being just us tonight." She looked at Jared with a smirk and was not going to mention that she was going to be with her dog.

"Oh, okay. Just thought I'd ask. Don't know til you try right?"

She stepped through the open door to escape the conversation. "Yep, you're right. See you around."

"Hope so" was all she heard as she went through the door and headed up the stairs.

Jenna shook her head, amazed at the troubles she was having with men and how comfortable she ended up feeling with Jared in such a short amount of time. He was one of those people she felt like she had known for a long time. He was easy to talk to and as she entered her room, she wished they'd talked longer. She had Shadow with her, but she wanted human companionship right now. The thought of being by herself made her feel isolated and lonely. She didn't want to start thinking about Keith *or* Neil. She came here to escape them.

As she grabbed a soda off the table she wondered if Jared would still be down in the hot tub or maybe swimming. But she'd already made it sound like she had a guy waiting for her. She knew it was a lost cause.

Later, after showering, she decided her and Shadow would go for a drive and check out the town a little. Maybe they could find a park for Shadow to stretch his legs and she could throw his ball for him to fetch.

They headed down the stairs to the lobby and as they turned the corner she saw Jared. He was wearing khaki shorts and a tied dye t-shirt with an old tattered cap and flip flops. He stood next to the counter and was asking the female clerk where a good restaurant was. Jenna watched as the hotel clerk, obviously attracted to Jared, tried to prolong the conversation. The employee played with her hair and batted her eyes at him. Then she tried to touch his hand, which was resting on the counter, and when that didn't work she frowned.

Jenna laughed to herself and then felt her face get warm. She knew she was at a crossroads and needed to decide if she was going to talk to him or if she would wait for him to leave. Just as she decided to turn back to go to her room, Jenna saw Jared turn towards her. He grinned.

He looked at her, then Shadow, then her again and started to laugh. "Is this the "he" you are with this evening? I must have really made a bad impression."

Jenna felt her face get even warmer but she smiled back. "No. You didn't make a bad impression. I just didn't want to be talked into something I didn't want to do."

"Oh, I see. Sorry if I made you feel uncomfortable. I told you my mouth gets ahead of my brain. I wasn't joking about that." He paused and then grinned at her like he had a secret. "So how are you feeling now?"

Jenna shook her head and smiled. It felt good to smile and there was no harm in a little company. "Okay, fine. But I'm driving and no funny stuff."

Jared looked at the lady behind the counter. "You hear that? I don't have to eat alone. Thanks for your help." The young woman slouched and glared at Jenna. Jared didn't seem to notice as he knocked on the countertop with his knuckles and turned away. He directed his attention to Jenna and opened the door for her and Shadow to pass through. "All right, I'm all yours. Hey. I just thought of something. What's your name?"

Jenna looked at him and laughed. "That's kind of funny. I'm Jenna and this is Shadow," she said and pointed down.

Jared looked down at Shadow. "Hmmm, a white dog named Shadow. Okay, it's your dog."

Jenna shook her head at his response as she thought of the first time Keith had met Shadow and was interested in his name. It amazed her how different Keith and Jared were already and she liked that. She smirked again and then put Keith to the back of her mind.

Finding a burger shack close by, they got some burgers and greasy fries and found a park close to the hotel. They picked a picnic table, not totally covered with bird droppings, and spread napkins down for a table cloth. Jenna fed Shadow a plain burger and then she devoured a cheeseburger and large fries for herself. Jared had a double burger with a pile of extras on it, and onion rings. He definitely was not afraid to eat in front of anyone.

When they were through they sat on top of the table and Jenna threw a ball for Shadow as her and Jared talked. She found out that he was originally from Minnesota and that he had recently moved to Delaware. He was single and had five brothers' and sisters' that were all living throughout the United States. He worked at an internet service and Jenna thought that his personality was perfect for working with the public.

The only thing Jenna said about herself was that she took pictures and then veered the conversation back to him. She was comfortable talking to Jared, but she didn't want to say too much about her personal life. He didn't seem to notice or care.

He told her some jokes and Jenna tried to tell him a few too. She messed up the end of every joke she told, and he laughed more at her than the jokes. Jenna laughed too.

The more they talked the more at ease she felt with him. It felt different than it had in the past, even with Keith. It felt normal to be with him, like Jared was a good friend. Jenna was perplexed but shrugged her shoulders and let the drama of Maryland fade. She felt like she could breathe again.

When the sun began to go down they went back to the hotel and she waved, said "bye" and headed up the steps.

"Now hold on a second. You can't just leave like that. I feel used," Jared said.

Jenna felt fear start to grow and she slowly turned back towards him. "Excuse me?"

"Well, we had fun didn't we? I was thinking. I wanted to check out the Amish community tomorrow. If I'm gonna be here, I might as well explore a little." His voice sounded almost shy. "Want to tag along?"

Jenna felt a sigh of relief and took a breath. "Oh, I'm sorry. I wasn't meaning to be rude." She paused and thought of what to say. "Yeah, I was being rude. I need to work on that." She leaned back on the wall. "Tomorrow? Sure, I'll tag along. I'll need to find somewhere for Shadow, though. I already need to find a place for Saturday."

"Saturday? What's Saturday?"

"Well, I did say I was here for work and pleasure. Saturday I have to work."

"Hmm. Don't tell me. You don't have to say what it is. I'll let my imagination work overtime."

Jenna rolled her eyes. After a short discussion they decided to meet at eleven in the lobby and she and Shadow headed up the stairs. Jenna didn't know where Jared had a room in the hotel, but he did not follow them and she was relieved.

# chapter 21

JENNA WOKE UP to feel more stress-free then she had in days. She couldn't help but to smile when she turned over in the bed and saw Shadow beside her, curled up in a ball asleep. She listened to his soft breathing momentarily before she got out of bed and started some coffee in the small machine on the dresser. She stretched and felt like she was being given a fresh start, again, and pulled open the curtains to feel the sunshine's warmth on her face.

After getting dressed and drinking half a cup of coffee, Jenna took Shadow outdoors to give him some relief from his full bladder. Smelling waffles as they came back in, Jenna wandered into the hotel's breakfast area and grabbed a muffin and juice on the way back to the room for a quick breakfast. She nibbled on her breakfast while she looked for a doggie daycare, for Shadow, for the next couple days and made reservations at a daycare close to the hotel.

She finished her juice and exhaled noisily as she dialed her phone to retrieve her messages. She didn't know what to expect and didn't know if Neil had found out her cell phone number too. Relieved, she heard the first message was from Keith, but then her body ached for him as she listened.

He said that he was worried about her and wanted her to get home safely from wherever it was she went. He told her that he missed her and didn't mean to get so upset the last time they had spoken. He sounded legitimately sorry and she almost wanted to drive home at that moment to be with him. However, at the same time, she knew she wasn't ready to handle that situation just yet. He had hurt her during their last conversation and she still felt the sting from his harsh words.

Though she hoped their relationship could be saved, she needed to work it out in her mind to make sure she made the right decision. She had made such a bad decision in the past and did not want to end up the same as she had been before. She couldn't, for her own sanity, and wouldn't for the same reason.

Jenna felt like she needed to change her future and forgive herself for her past. She felt that she needed to be a strong woman to make the clear choice based on facts and not the desire to be held in his arms. She felt like she was still in a transformation, like the Pipevine Swallowtail went through its life cycle, to become the best woman she could. And, right now, she didn't want an outside influence to sway her from this. She had a big choice to make.

Jenna sighed and listened to the second message from Kathy. She thought Kathy sounded concerned when she mentioned that Keith had called her. She told Jenna that she thought Keith was a good man and she thought Jenna should give him a chance.

Jenna was impressed that he went to such lengths to get a hold of her. She didn't know that Keith even knew John and Kathy's last name. Nonetheless, she still was not ready to talk to him or make a decision.

After she listened to the messages, she decided to try and call Kathy but got her answering machine instead. Almost relived by this, she told Kathy she was fine and was going to go check out some sites and to not worry about her. But Jenna couldn't bring herself to tell Kathy that she would be with another man and felt guilty.

Jenna hung up the phone and brushed through her hair. As she combed through the tangles, she tried come up with the right thing to do about her predicament. She couldn't decide what would be the right option to make her happy and to feel safe at the same time. Then she thought of Jared.

The objective side of her mind was saying to not see Jared and concentrate on the task of Keith and Neil. There was already too much on her platter and she was getting into more than she could handle.

But the pleasurable side of her mind said to go for the day. Everyone needed a break and there was no harm in having some fun. She had been helping everyone but herself lately. And in the end, everyone needed to relax and enjoy the unexpected every now and again.

Though, in the past she had always told Kathy everything and not telling her about Jared made it all feel wrong. But what was she to do? It would be rude to bail on their plans today without being rude to him. She almost felt obligated to spend the day sightseeing with him, or was that just an excuse to go?

Jenna tapped her feet on the carpeted floor while trying to figure out the right way to go. She weighed the choices of spending the day alone or spending the day with someone she felt comfortable with, like a friend. Standing up, she grabbed the piece of paper with the reservation for Shadow and knew what she was going to do.

Jared seemed to have an easygoing personality and was fun to talk to. She was comfortable with him and was actually looking forward to spending the day with him. Of course she felt a little remorse for hanging out with another man, but she didn't want to be alone. Besides, Jared never gave the impression of wanting anything more from her.

Around ten in the morning, Jenna headed to take Shadow to his play date. The lady who ran the daycare seemed very sweet and Shadow liked her too. She showed Jenna around and led Shadow into a windowed room with numerous other dogs that were playing and chewing on toys. Shadow entered the room and instantly began to wrestle and play with the other dogs. Jenna knew he was safe and happy and felt comfortable leaving him.

When Jenna arrived back at the hotel, Jared was waiting in the lobby. He was sitting in an overstuffed chair, staring at the wall in front of him while he tapped his foot on the floor. He wore plaid shorts and an orange t-shirt. His tennis shoes looked new and his black hair was covered mostly by a baseball cap. He looked annoyed and she wondered if the day wouldn't be as good as she had thought it would be.

"Jared?"

He turned his head and looked at her, surprised. "Hey, I thought you left without me."

Jenna stepped in front of him and wrinkled her forehead, confused. "Why'd you think that?"

"Because your car was gone when I looked outside a few minutes ago."

She giggled. "I had to take Shadow for a play date." She looked down at her watch. "It's not even eleven o'clock yet."

Jared thumped himself on the side of his head. "Well, don't I feel dumb."

Jenna felt appreciated. "I'm ready to go if you are." She headed to the door. "I'll drive."

They headed outside and after a short drive they arrived at an Amish community. Jared paid for them to take a tour on a horse and buggy ride. Jenna giggled like a little kid as the horse began to pull the buggy and she saw Jared smile too.

She instantly felt a sense of innocence as she watched children play and a large windmill turn slowly on top of a hill. As they moved down the road they talked about how quiet it was and watched as some horses pulled a plow in a far-off field.

The day was gorgeous with a soft breeze to fight off the heat of the sun. A few large clouds were motionless in the sky and fields of flowers moved with the breeze. The horses' hooves began to sound like a rhythm of a song as they clicked and clacked on the road. Even the guide's voice seemed at ease and happy to be where he was as he told them about the community.

The guide took them to a couple of roadside stores and Jenna was fascinated with the workmanship of everything from key-chains to kitchen tables. She fell in love with the intricate detail of the quilts, which the women of the community had made, and had to buy one to take home. Then at the next store they visited, Jenna found a cute birdhouse that she thought would be perfect in her backyard.

After they were done with the tour they went to try some Dutch cooking that their guide had said was popular in the area. They found the restaurant he had suggested and sat across from one another at a table. The smells of the food made Jenna hungry.

She looked at Jared and saw a strange expression on his face. "What?"

"Oh, nothing. It's just been such an awesome day. You're pretty awesome yourself." He paused and smirked. "Well, except for that hideous blanket you bought."

Jenna gave him a look of disbelief. "What? Ugly? You're crazy. First, it's a quilt, not a blanket. And second, it's beautiful."

He shrugged his shoulders. "I'm just kidding you but, really, you are pretty awesome."

She grabbed her glass of water and twirled the ice cubes in the glass. "Thank you. I think you are pretty cool too. I like to be around you. It's been nice to have your company."

"Yeah, I know, I'm a pretty fun guy to have around," he said and sat back in his chair. Then he looked at her with a serious face. "So can we … "

Jenna stopped him mid-sentence. She felt her heart beat hard and did not want the day spoiled with him trying to press her for something further than friendship. She put her hand up as if she were stopping a car. "Whoa. I really like hanging around you, Jared, but … Really I just wanted some company today. There is nothing more than that." She placed her folded hands on top of his. "Can we please just enjoy the dinner and leave it at that?"

Jared gently pulled his hands from under hers and folded them in front of him. "Wow. Hey, umm, can I finish my sentence? I was going to ask if we could stay for dessert or if you had to go get your dog."

Jenna felt foolish and could feel her face turn red. "I feel stupid."

Jared took a drink of his ice tea. "Hey, it's okay. I understand. Women always get that impression of me."

She looked puzzled. "No, I … "

Jared cut in. "I'm not trying to rush anything here. I've enjoyed this day and frankly don't want it to end. I just didn't know what time you had to pick your dog up."

Jenna took a bite of a breadstick and wished she hadn't said anything. "After we are done eating I'll have to go get Shadow but I'm sure there's time for dessert."

Jenna looked down embarrassed. She knew she had jumped to conclusions with Jared. She had said things that had ruined the mood and she didn't want to do that. Not today.

She had mixed emotions for Jared and was confused. She felt comfortable with him like a best friend, but she also found him attractive and felt little twinges of desire. She didn't know she could feel attracted to someone so soon after being hurt by Keith. Or maybe she felt that way because of what had happened before she left. Maybe she was desperate for affection.

Taking another bite of her breadstick, she put Keith to the back of her mind and looked at Jared's dimples as he smiled. He really had handsome facial features and his eyes sparkled when he talked. "Jared, you have … "

"And here's your food. I hope you find everything to be delicious. Enjoy," the waitress said as she placed their food on the table.

Jenna forgot what she was going to say and stared at the food. Some of the Dutch cooking she had never tasted or ever thought of tasting.

They started with a bowl of chicken corn soup with breadsticks and then Jenna had a homemade chicken pot pie. Jared's meal was a huge plate of meatloaf with a side of chow chow.

They enjoyed the meal and tasted food from each other's plates to try all of the different flavors. Meatloaf had never been one of Jenna's favorites but this one was moist and delicious and she stole a couple extra pieces when Jared wasn't looking. When it came to the chow chow, they both hesitated but found out it was pickled vegetables. Neither had ever tasted anything like it before and found it to be pretty tasty.

Everything was comfort food and good to eat. When the waitress came back to ask if they wanted dessert, Jenna declined. Jared rubbed his stomach and decided there was still room to try some of the famous Shoo Fly Pie.

While they waited, they laughed about the pie and tried to guess how it got its name. When the plate was brought to the table, Jared devoured the entire piece of pie and made sounds of pleasure with every bite.

Shortly after dinner they picked up Shadow and headed back to the hotel. They pulled into the parking lot and Jenna felt like she was a teenager on a first date. She felt awkward and didn't know what to say or do.

After parking her car and turning off the engine, Jared leaned over casually and kissed her on the cheek. Suddenly, Jenna felt desperation to be held and touched. She turned towards Jared and his expression gave the impression that he felt the same way. He looked at her with desire and leaned towards her slowly. She suddenly felt lightheaded, like she had drank too much wine and leaned to kiss him. Instantly, she felt guilty but pushed it away.

His mouth was hot and addictive. The kisses quickly became passionate and their bodies leaned in the seats to be closer. He put his fingers through her hair and then moved them down to her shoulders and then her back. The feel of his hands on her body made her crave more and she was ready to climb over the seat to be closer to him. Just then, she heard Shadow whimper in the back seat and she pulled away.

She suddenly felt claustrophobic. "I need to get out of this car."

He wiped his hand across his mouth. "Saved by the dog, huh?"

Jenna looked out the window and felt embarrassed as she watched a family of five get into a van a few cars away. She didn't know if anyone had seen them kiss, but the thought of it made her feel childish and ashamed. "I didn't even kiss anyone in a parking lot as a teenager."

Jared looked around and took a deep breath. "I guess there's a first for everything, right? I really like you. I want to get to know you better. I want to get to know the real Jenna."

When Jared said that last sentence Jenna's mind went straight to Keith. He had said those words too and look where it had ended up. She suddenly felt defensive and trapped. Just moments ago she wanted to be close to Jared but now she wanted to run away. One sentence had sent her mood to a different place.

All she could think about was Keith and how he hurt her and his cold eyes the last time she saw him. His words had cut her like a knife. But then she started to remember the sweet things he had said, before that night, that had made her feel special.

Jenna pictured Keith's arms around her and his hand in hers. Thinking back she could see his hazel eyes as they looked at her sweetly and she remembered their first kiss. It was that same day that he had asked to know the real her.

She remembered how she had felt that day. Keith made her feel safe and she wanted to learn to trust him. But now she was in a car with another man and had just kissed him.

"What am I doing?" Jenna asked out loud.

Jared put his head back against the seat. "From the look of your expression, I think you are going to tell me that this is wrong and you have to go. Am I right?"

She took a deep breath and grabbed the steering wheel with both hands and squeezed. She looked out the windshield and watched as a group of birds flew by with ease. Their wings glided on the air and she wished she was that free.

"I'm sorry. I'm actually in a relationship, well kind of. We had a fight and I don't know what is going to happen. But, just now, I realized I like him more than I ever thought I did. I'm sorry." Jenna said as she looked intently out of the windshield, afraid to look at Jared.

She heard Jared move in the seat next to her, and he made a loud sigh. Reluctantly, she looked over at him. He was shaking his head from side to side.

He made another sighing noise before he spoke. "Classic. Just classic. I find a beautiful woman by herself and she shuts me down. Just my luck."

"I really am sorry. I enjoy your company, but I'm not ready to go further than that." Jenna's hands started to shake. She squeezed the steering wheel tighter to help control her emotions. She knew she was going to cry and tried to keep it from happening by closing her eyes tight. A tear still passed through, onto her cheek. Surprised, she felt Jared's hand softly wipe the tear away.

Jared turned his body towards hers and spoke softly. "Hey, it's all right. I'm not mad. If anything I'm sad. You really are wonderful but I don't want to confuse you any more than you are already." He slapped his hands on his knees and made Jenna jump in her seat. "Jenna, I'm going to go so that you don't feel uncomfortable. Maybe I'll see you later and we can talk."

He didn't give her a chance to respond and got out of the car, shutting the door softly. When Jenna looked in the side mirror, she could see him walk towards the hotel with his head down and his hands in his pockets.

Jenna heard Shadow jump into the empty seat beside her. She looked at him and he put a paw on her arm. He let out a small whimper and she hugged him and let the rest of her tears spill onto her cheeks.

# chapter 22

THE DARKENING SKY made the shadows seem long and ominous. The street was filled with them and they were different shades of gray as they seemed to get closer every second. Jenna's steps hastened as the streetlights began to blink. The house seemed to get further away with every step she took. Her heart pounded in her chest and her breath seemed heavy. Her eyes darted around the street and she saw a shadow moving faster than the rest. It was trying to reach her. The porch light was just in front of her so she started to run towards it. She could not see the ground from steam rising from it and tripped on a branch. Tumbling onto the ground she turned quickly to look behind her. The shadow grew larger as it moved swiftly towards her.

She felt a scream in her throat but it wouldn't escape her lips. Thrusting her legs and feet against the grass she tried to edge closer to the house. But the grass was wet and she kept sliding without making any progress. The shadow was almost on top of her and she put her arms in front of her to try and protect herself. Then, suddenly, a bright light sliced through the fog and the shadow let out a screech of anger before it disappeared.

Protecting her eyes, she squinted through them, half closed, to look into the light. She could see a large form approaching. She tried to escape but felt a hand grab her arm. Terrified from the touch, she pulled away and looked towards the form. As her eyes adjusted to the light she could see the figure before her. It was Keith. He had saved her from the shadows. He helped her stand and held her in his arms.

Jenna's eyes opened, remembering the dream. She was hugging a pillow tightly and she smelled it, expecting to smell Keith's cologne. He had felt so close and she swore he was in the room with her. She strained to listen for any sound of another person and groaned when she did not and knew it was just a dream.

The thought of him with her made her happy and she stretched under the warm blankets. Nestled in them like a cocoon, she pulled the blankets around her neck procrastinating against the start of a new day.

The last thing she wanted to do right now was to get out of the warm bed and start the day. Just to lounge around and watch television seemed so tantalizing instead of going to a battle reenactment. It was nice to feel safe and warm under the covers with Shadow snoozing away beside her.

As she stretched again she looked at the clock and frowned, knowing she would have to get up. In all her years of taking pictures, she had never missed an appointment and wasn't going to start today, although the idea of seeing Jared on the battlefield made her uncomfortable.

She covered her head with a pillow and screamed into it. She thought about the past couple days and couldn't believe she had spent so much time with him. What was she doing letting another man into her life? She already had enough trouble and she added another scenario to the mix. Sometimes she could not understand how she got into these situations but this time she had allowed Jared into her life and created the mess herself.

How would she ever tell Keith? Her stomach twisted into a knot when she thought about the expression he would have on his face. She had been so scared that Keith would hurt her, but in the end she was the one who would hurt him.

Jenna turned over in the blankets and glanced at her phone on the dresser. It seemed so small and unimportant but it played such a vital part in her life. It was her lifeline to the world but it had not rung much lately. She noticed there was no blinking light for any messages for her and frowned and wondered why Keith had only left one.

What if he didn't want to talk things out when she got back home? Would she be able to go back to the way she had before Keith came into her life? What would Keith do or say when he found out about Neil?

Her life was so crazy right now and the only norm was Shadow. Jenna rolled over on her side and watched him sleep. Staring at him, she wondered what Shadow would say about her situation if he could talk. She needed someone to lead her in the right direction and she thought he knew her best.

Jenna moaned and was exhausted when she thought about the men in her life. Within a few weeks she had gone from having not one man in her life to having three. They were so distressing and she didn't know what do to about them. Each one troubled her in a different way.

Jared was a nice guy and she really enjoyed being around him. She didn't feel the tension like she was on a date or that he did either. He was so easy to talk to and he made her smile. But so did Keith.

Keith had let her tell him about her dark past and never judged her for it. He had held her hand and made her believe she was safe. Keith tried to make her happy even if he wasn't comfortable, like on the Ferris wheel. Jenna didn't get the impression from Jared that he would be that devoted.

With Jared she didn't feel anything but a moment of lust. If she had stayed with him it would have only been to use him for a body to hold her. He may not have minded, but she would have. She suddenly felt dirty thinking about it.

She kicked her legs under the blankets and was ashamed when she thought about Keith and Jared. She had tried to justify being with Jared because Keith had been so mean, but in the end she was wrong and thoughtless.

She should have talked to Keith when she had first arrived in Pennsylvania. When she first heard his message, which seemed sincere, she should have called him at that moment. But he hadn't called at all yesterday and she would be too busy until later tonight.

Finally, when her thoughts went to Neil, she cringed. She closed her eyes and tried to push the thought of him away. He was the worst of all.

Keeping her eyes closed as tight as she could, Jenna wished she could fall back asleep. But even though she wanted to stay in bed, she needed to get moving and groaned at the notion.

She knew she would just have to dodge Jared at the hotel and now at the war reenactment too. The only good thing she had going was that she had never told him she would be there, so he wouldn't be looking for her. Hopefully she would get through the day and he would be gone from her life forever.

After throwing off the covers and stepping onto the floor, she tried to shake off all of her anxieties. She needed to get prepared. Since earlier she had decided to be at the battlefield to get pictures of them setting up first thing in the morning.

The contract was very important to her and she wanted to get a large assortment of images to present to them. Maybe they would ask her back next year too. The idea of it made her grin.

After Jenna took Shadow outside and was back in her room she lingered in the shower. The hot water felt good and she wished it could wash all her troubles away. The pressure of the water pulsated against her face and she held her breath. She lowered her head and watched as water fell from the ends of her hair and ran down to the bottom of the shower to escape down the drain.

By the time she got out of the shower, the mirror was steamed up and she wiped it with her hand. Water droplets formed on the mirror and she looked past them and stared at the face looking back. She started to see herself differently.

After just a few short weeks, she did not quite look like a scared woman anymore. She looked stronger and seemed to have more self-esteem. She had Keith to thank for some of it, but some had come from having to confront her fears. And the worst of her fears was Neil.

The idea of seeing Neil made her shiver. She never thought he would come back into her life, or at least she had hoped he wouldn't. The miles from Idaho had given her a fake sense of security. She was going to have to confront the problem eventually. Staying in Pennsylvania forever was not an option.

One thing for sure, she really wanted to take care of it without Keith finding out. She didn't want him to think she was using him as a bodyguard. Things were bad enough already.

Jenna looked at the clock and saw the time for the battle reenactment was getting close. She had to stop thinking about everything else but the battle she needed to take pictures of. She had to get in the right frame of mind to get the job done right. Her bag with everything she needed was ready to go and she and Shadow headed out the door.

Arriving at the site, after dropping Shadow off at doggie daycare, Jenna looked around and was astounded by the view. Hundreds of men and women were walking around, some in costume and others still in shorts and tank tops. There were horses being groomed and tents being erected. There were tables of refreshments and make up being put on anxious faces.

In the distance she heard the sound of a musket and saw the accompanying puff of smoke. Union and Confederate flags waved in the breeze and cannons were moved onto the field. Drummer boys practiced their cadence and she approved of their cute uniforms.

After a few minutes of looking around, Jenna grabbed her camera and started to capture as much as she could. The first photo she took was of a man dressed as a general. He stood with a lit cigar in his hand and his head was tipped back in a heartfelt laugh. Jenna thought the picture was perfection with the soft smoke from his cigar contrasted against the deep, intense wrinkles around the man's eyes. She imagined the photo in black in white to portray the contrast even more.

Right after she took the first photo she couldn't snap the pictures fast enough. She wanted to capture the entire story of the battle and everything that happened to make it realistic. There was so much activity and she didn't know which direction to turn first.

By the time the fictitious battle began, she had already taken hundreds of pictures. After she took a minute to rest, she watched as the spectators lined up and the soldiers had their last pep talks before it all began. She wondered if she would be able to pick Jared out of the crowd of blue and gray but knew that it would be impossible.

A bugle rang out in the distance and then drummer boys began to play their song. There were hundreds of horses and when they began to run, the sound of their thundering hooves gave Jenna goose bumps. The horses began to whinny and snort and men began to yell. Gunshots rang out and men fell to the ground grasping their chests. Jenna was impressed by the actors' portrayal and caught as much as she could with her camera.

It seemed to be hours before the North was celebrating their victory. Jenna took a deep breath and was proud of herself for taking on such a large task. She watched as the last clouds of smoke, from cannons, dispersed into the afternoon air and was pleased.

The spectators clapped and hollered their approval while the generals on horseback, tipped their hats as they walked by. People scattered within moments after the battle was complete and the spectators disappeared as quickly as they had emerged. Jenna continued to take pictures, wanting to tell the entire story. She stayed until the last horse was loaded into a trailer and their owner drove away.

After looking back one last time, Jenna headed back to her car and noticed a figure leaning on the hood. As she moved closer she saw Jared and felt annoyed. She didn't want the wonderful day to be tarnished with any more emotional drama.

As he came into closer view Jenna could tell he was sweating from the costume he had worn. He was wearing casual shorts and t-shirt with the same baseball cap she had seen him wear yesterday. Handsome or not, she didn't want to deal with him right now.

Jared stood up and wiped his forehead as she approached. "You're a sight for sore eyes. I didn't think I'd ever see you again. What are you doing here?"

Jenna raised her bag containing her camera. "I was here to take pictures of the battle."

"Huh. Why didn't you tell me that when we first met and I told you that I would be here? Never mind. Don't answer that. I didn't even see you but I did see your car when I was going to leave." He patted the hood of her car. "It tends to stand out a bit."

Jenna wiped some of the perspiration off the back of her neck. "Yeah, it does get attention. I don't know what the big deal is. It's just a car."

Jared raised his eyebrows and studied the car's curves like it was a woman. "It's just … Really? This is a sweet ride."

Jenna rolled her eyes and smiled. Every time a man walked by her car, they would look at it like it was a gorgeous woman that had everything they desired. She never understood why they felt that way and knew she never would. She just shook her head and looked at Jared. "So did you die right away? What side did you play on?"

Jared looked back at Jenna and had a grin on his face. He puffed out his chest before he spoke. "I was a barefooted Confederate. I lasted the majority of the battle. I was finally shot in the belly and left for dead."

She batted her eyes at him. "Oh, I'm so sorry."

Jared took off his cap and wiped sweat off his forehead before putting it back on. "Yeah, I bet you are. How are you, anyway?"

Jenna kicked at a dandelion that was trying to grow through the packed soil. "Confused. Ashamed."

"Yeah, come on. You're fine. It would be hard for any woman not to fall for me." He said and sounded vain.

She rolled her eyes. "Yeah, right. It doesn't help that I did. It confuses me more."

"Don't sweat it. You made it clear this other guy has your heart. I understand. I just wanted to tell you there are no hard feelings."

Jenna wrinkled her brow and looked up at him. "You're right. I have given him my heart. I didn't realize that until you said it." She stepped past him and got into her car. "Jared, you're a great guy, but I've got to go." As she went to close the door she looked at Jared with approval. "I really hope you find a good woman to be with. She would be lucky to have you in her life."

Jared put his hand on the door, preventing it from shutting. "Jenna, if I ever find another woman like you I won't let her get away. I'll sweep her off her feet and marry her." He moved his hand and let the door close. He stepped back, put his hands in his pockets, and smiled.

Jenna drove off without looking back and had one thing on her mind. She had to talk to Keith and tell him she was falling in love.

# chapter 23

KATHY DRIED A plate from the sink and put it down when the phone rang. "Hello?"

"Kathy, hi, it's Jenna."

"Sweetie, I'm so happy to hear from you."

Jenna spoke fast and excited. "Yeah, I'm happy to talk to you too. Have you talked to Keith? Is he mad at me? I have to know before I talk to him so I know what to expect."

Kathy sat down in a chair and rubbed the dishtowel against a scratch in the table. "Yes, I'm doing fine also. Thank you for asking."

Jenna frowned. "Kathy. I'm sorry. I just need to know what he said."

Kathy paused a moment before she spoke. "Well, he is worried about you and upset with how he spoke to you." She paused again. "I know you don't want to hear it but … he confronted Neil."

Jenna stood up from her chair and started to pace the carpet in her hotel room. "He did what? When? How?"

Kathy closed her eyes. "Keith went to find you and Neil was at your house snooping around. Keith didn't really say too much about it. We're all worried. It took a lot for him to track our phone number down. That should say a lot. He really does care about you. He was pretty upset but I talked him down and helped him understand the situation. He's worried about you as much as us. Keith is a good man."

Jenna couldn't believe this was happening. She couldn't believe Neil had found her and now Keith was involved. She wanted to scream and cry at the same time. Her hands started to shake and she felt perspiration on her back.

"What do I do? How do I say sorry to Keith for all of this? How do I take care of it? I didn't want Keith to even know about Neil being around. I wanted to take care of it myself. Everything is ruined. Ruined!"

"Jenna calm down dear. I don't know. I do know you don't have to tell Keith you're sorry. He's worried about you, not mad at you."

"I have messed everything up. Keith was so good to me and now with Neil and Jared. I feel so frustrated and defeated."

"Jared? Who's Jared?"

Jenna fell back onto the bed and Shadow licked her arm. Jenna felt deflated. "He was a guy I met here. It didn't go anywhere but I still feel guilty." Tears ran down her cheeks and she didn't bother to wipe them away.

"Jenna, it's okay to talk to other men. There's no law against it."

"I know, but I spent the whole day with him yesterday and we kissed." Jenna paused and tried to control her emotions. "But I stopped it and felt horrible for even putting myself in that situation."

Kathy didn't answer for a moment. "I don't know what to say. I do have to that I'm surprised by your actions. There has been a lot going on with you lately. But the Jared thing, that's between you and Keith now."

The room looked blurry through the tears on Jenna's eyelashes. She took a deep breath and rubbed her eyes to try and clear her vision. "My life is so messed up but I'll have to face it and make it right. I'm done with my job here and I'm going to head home right now. I'll figure out what to do on the way."

Kathy said, "Why don't you drive home tomorrow? Call Keith today but don't drive with so many emotions affecting you. I don't want anything bad to happen."

Jenna suddenly heard John's gruff voice as he got on the phone. "Jenna. It's John. Now you quit worrying about so much. We'll help you get through this. We consider you family and we're not going to let anything bad happen. Keep your chin up and drive safely when you come home."

Hearing John's voice gave Jenna a sense of security. He spoke sternly but affectionately. She felt more tears stream down her face but was happy with the thought of such good people in her life. Kathy got back on the phone and said how much she loved her and hung up.

Jenna reached over to Shadow and scratched him behind the ears. "Well, boy. We better learn how to get tough quick. We're gonna need it." Jenna dialed Keith's phone number.

"Jenna, is that you?" Keith's voice sounded worried and relieved.

"Yes, it's me. Kathy told me about ... " She had to swallow to keep from crying again. "She told me about Neil. I'm sorry. I wanted to tell you."

"Stop. Don't say sorry again. You have nothing to be sorry for. I do!" His voice got softer as he continued. "I need to say sorry to you. You tried to talk to me. You came to me and I pushed you away. I'm sorry."

Jenna listened to Keith's words and twirled her hair on her finger. His voice sounded comforting and she wished he was there to hold her. He sounded so close like he was in the next room. She started to sob as she spoke. "I miss you so much. My life is so messed up and I never wanted to drag you into the craziness of it."

"Well, it looks like I'm part of it and we'll get through it together. That is, if you still want me to be part of it." He sounded hesitant and scared.

"Oh my gosh! Yes!" Jenna almost screamed. "Yes I want you in my life. I don't remember what it was like before you, except empty. You've become so much to me and I think I'm ... wait." Jenna thought of Jared and she was not going to get back into the relationship without Keith knowing the truth. "I have to tell you something."

"What is it?" Keith said with hesitance in his voice.

Jenna closed her eyes and tried to calm herself. "I met a guy while I was here. He was really nice but nothing serious happened. We spent time together but I did kiss him."

The silence that followed made Jenna's ears ring. Her heart was pounding and she felt sweaty. This was the most nervous she had been her entire life. She didn't know if Keith was on the phone or if he hung up. It seemed an eternity before he spoke again.

"Oh. I see. I don't know what to say, Jenna. Does he mean something to you?"

Jenna could tell from Keith's voice that she had hurt him badly. She wiped her eyes and bit her lip. "Keith, it wasn't like you and me. It was more of a ... I don't know. It didn't feel right. I stopped it from going any further. I told him about you."

"That was it?"

"Yes, that was it. I wanted to tell you. I don't want to keep anything from you. I am falling in love with you." By time she was done speaking it was almost a whisper.

She couldn't believe the explosion she felt throughout her body when she said the words to him. It was like she had been buried under ground and saying those words pushed her back to the surface. She meant what she said and liked how it sounded coming from her lips. She prayed she would hear it from him some day too.

"Jenna, I only have one more thing to say."

She felt her body go tense and prepared herself for the worst.

Keith spoke softly. "I want you to get home so I can hold you again."

A smile filled Jenna's face and she kicked her feet on the bed with excitement. Her heart felt like it might burst. They were being given a second chance and she couldn't wait to start.

# chapter 24

THE WIND BLEW through Jenna's hair as she cruised down the highway. She pressed down on the accelerator and could not wait to get home. She felt like she had been gone for a few weeks, instead of a few days, and needed to be close to the people she loved.

Listening to the radio, Jenna paid close attention to the words a woman sang about not letting a past relationship make her weak. The woman said that going through what she had, had made her a fighter instead, and Jenna thought the song seemed to refer to her and her life. She tried to memorize the chorus, about being a stronger woman, and knew she had become a stronger woman too.

She reached over and ruffed up the hair on Shadow's back and then saw a road sign for her exit to head home. She was going to be there in less than ten minutes and felt excited to be so close. After thinking for a moment she decided to go straight to Keith's apartment and hopefully have a good experience, unlike the last time. As she pulled into the parking lot her body seemed to come alive and she couldn't wait to see him. She grabbed her phone and called him. "Hey, what are you doing?"

"I'm waiting for you. When will you get home? Where are you at?"

"Well, I'm in the parking lot in front of your building. I was wondering if we could sneak Shadow in."

"You're here?! I'm on my way down."

Keith went bursting through the door barefoot and almost ran to Jenna's car. She didn't even have a chance to open her door as he swung it open. He grabbed her arm and pulled her out as she laughed. He hugged her close in his arms and breathed in her perfume. He kissed her neck, ears, cheek, and finally her mouth. He kissed her hard.

Jenna couldn't believe her exhilaration when she saw him come through the door. He kissed her with desperation and passion and she melted in his arms. His kiss sent shivers down her back and she did not want it to end. Her stomach felt like it had a hundred butterflies dancing in it and she suddenly felt drunk.

Keith pulled back and looked into her eyes. "Hello."

Jenna had to lean back on her car to not fall over. Her legs felt weak and her head was spinning. She stared into his eyes but couldn't speak. Tears took the place of words and she hugged him again. With her head on his shoulder she whispered. "I love you, Keith."

Keith pulled back again, looked at her, and then kissed her with passion. He let her go and spoke softly. "I'm sorry for hurting you. Please forgive me."

"I forgive you. Do you forgive me?"

"Of course." Keith softly pushed her towards the rear of the car. He leaned into the interior, grabbed a leash, and attached it to Shadow's collar as Shadow wiggled with excitement. "Let's go inside."

They entered the building and took the stairs up to the second floor. Keith said something about the elevator but Jenna felt like she was in a daze and couldn't hear very well at that moment.

He opened the door to his apartment and Jenna saw boxes stacked against a wall. The only furniture was a couch with a coffee table next to it. The whole space looked untidy but that did not concern her right then. She wanted the man standing in front of her and she wanted him now.

Shadow jumped on the couch and sniffed around, laid down, and seemed comfortable already. Jenna watched him get cozy and then grabbed Keith's hand and led him in the direction of what she imagined was the bedroom.

Keith followed her with no objection and let her be in control. Jenna walked past the bathroom and decided the room with the fewest boxes in it was his bedroom. They entered the room, hand in hand, and as they went just past the door Jenna turned towards him. She looked into his eyes and began to unbutton his shirt. She let out a small moan as she looked down at his bare chest and watched his stomach move with deep, heavy breaths. Her hand ran down his stomach, across his abs, and slowly moved to his jeans. She looked up to see his eyes close and knew he was enjoying the moment. In the meantime she released the button and unzipped his jeans watching his expression the entire time.

Keith let out a sigh as Jenna's hands pushed down the material and ran her fingers across his hips. He finished removing his jeans and briefs and then opened his eyes as Jenna pushed him back to the bed. He sat at the edge and looked at her with hunger in his eyes.

Jenna stepped back so he could have a full view of her body and began to undress. Her hands moved slowly and provocatively across the material. She watched Keith's face with every button she opened and as her clothes fell, one piece at a time, to the floor.

She stepped closer and all she could think was having his mouth and tongue on her flesh. And all she could hear was Keith's breathing through the silence of the room.

Keith's breath quickened as Jenna moved within inches of him and another moan passed his lips. He touched her waist and then slowly moved his hands up to her belly and then up to her breasts.

Jenna closed her eyes and saw white flashes of light behind her eyelids and felt a heat come over her. She felt his hands continue up to her neck and face. He ran his fingers through her hair and then began to move back down with precision. He touched every inch of her and she did not know if she could handle much more.

When she looked at him, his eyes met hers and Jenna moaned just seeing the appetite in his gaze. She wanted to taste his flesh and then feel it against hers. Keith seemed to sense what she wanted and pushed back further onto the bed, laying on his back, ready for her.

Like a panther, towards its prey, Jenna moved slowly, until she was on top of him. Her fingers touched his chest and then followed with her mouth. Everywhere her fingers slid across, she followed with her tongue. She heard moans of approval and tasted sweat from the heat building in him.

After what seemed centuries of kissing, Keith flipped her on the bed so he was on top. He did the same ritual of touching and kissing and licking her flesh. Then he turned Jenna on her stomach and within seconds, she could feel his fingertips tracing the outline of her tattoo. He moved up from the tattoo and ran his hand up and down her spine kissing her back all the while. He turned her again and kissed her stomach. Her back arched to be closer to him.

When Keith put the weight of his body on top of her, she almost screamed for him to be even closer. Her fingers dug into his back and she had to fight the urge to run her fingernails hard against him. The built up passion was past the point of return. It didn't matter if a phone rang or an earthquake started, she was not going to quit until she was satisfied. She wanted Keith to be just as satisfied as her, and she moved beneath him to show her anticipation.

He teased her by moving his hips and pulling back on her hair so she would raise her chin to taste his mouth. He looked at her with anticipation and she knew the time had finally come. At that moment he thrust into her with an aching pleasure. They both gasped against their rising ecstasy.

Keith felt so good and Jenna did not want their time together to end. It was beyond anything she had felt in her entire life. He put his hands in hers, above her head, and put his lips on hers with a moan. Time escaped them as their bodies moved together and were meant to be as one.

Jenna's body was on fire from her head down to her toes. And after what seemed hours of pure pleasure, they both released and she swore she felt the earth move below them.

Keith fell to the side of her and they both tried to catch their breath. After a few minutes Keith propped himself up on his elbow and ran his other hand over Jenna's belly. He looked at her entire body and then spoke, soft and sensual. "Are you going to stay with me for the rest of the day?"

Jenna turned her body towards his. "Of course. I'm not going anywhere."

Keith put his arm around her and they both fell into a blissful sleep, side by side.

Later they were wakened by a whimpering from the edge of the bed. Keith stretched under the raveled blankets and then playfully touched Jenna's face, making her purr. He sat up and started to dress. "You stay and sleep. I'll slip Shadow outside for a while."

Jenna just smiled. She pulled the blankets over her body and then covered her head with a pillow. When she heard the door to the apartment close she remained under the blankets but uncovered her head to look around the bedroom. She let out a small sound of disbelief from the lack of personality it showed.

The room had a bed, of course, a dresser and a nightstand. Besides the lamp and an alarm clock the room was mostly bare. The walls were beige and the trim work was a darker color of the same beige along with brown curtains over the windows. Jenna thought it looked very cold and disconnected without any pictures on the walls or any other personal touches. But as she raised her head she saw the picture Keith had taken of her on the beach. It was propped up on the dresser next to an open bottle of water. Jenna couldn't help but grin seeing her picture in his bedroom.

Reluctantly she got out of the warm bed and headed to the bathroom. When she was done she grabbed a t-shirt, from Keith's dresser, and put it over her naked body. She walked back down the hallway and looked inquisitively around the rest of the apartment. She rolled her eyes at the impersonal feeling the apartment gave compared to her own home.

Thirsty, she entered the kitchen, went to the refrigerator and grabbed a bottle of water. The cold liquid tasted good on her throat and satisfied her thirst. She enjoyed a few more drinks before she went into the living room and laid down on the couch to wait for Keith. Her eyes soon grew heavy and she dozed off with her head on a wadded up blanket.

Within a few minutes, Keith came back into the apartment and his eyes went straight to Jenna, on the couch, curled up like a cat. He stood and watched her sleep and Jenna's eyes fluttered open when Shadow licked her hand. She grinned.

Keith grinned back at her. "Well, hello, sleepy head."

Jenna stretched on the couch and let out a lazy moan. She felt skin being uncovered as she stretched but was not embarrassed showing herself to him. She watched Keith look at her and it made her feel beautiful and loved. "Hey, you. Hope it's all right I stole a shirt," she said lazily.

"It's just become my favorite shirt." He smirked. "I might need it back later."

She pulled on the edge of the shirt. "Oh, really. You want it back now?"

Keith came to the couch and sat down beside her. "No, not right now, but you have to promise something."

"What's that?" Jenna asked and tilted her head to one side.

He put his head next to hers so their noses were almost touching. "You only wear it when I'm around to see."

"I think I can do that. It's a deal." Jenna said and gave him a kiss to finalize the contract.

Keith fell on the couch and snuggled next to her. The rest of the afternoon and evening was lazy and perfect. The majority of the time they were cuddled together as they watched movies from the couch. They giggled, tickled, and caressed the entire day. Keith ordered a pizza which ended up being a late lunch and dinner. Neither of them wanted to leave his apartment. They did not want to ruin the spell the day had created.

As Jenna took the last bite of the pizza, Keith turned so that their knees were touching. He took her hands in his and looked at her seriously. "Jenna, we need to talk."

Jenna smiled at him. "Well, if you wanted the last piece of pizza, it's too late. It's in my tummy already."

"No, we need to talk about something important."

Jenna saw that he was serious and frowned. "What?"

Keith squeezed her hands and looked down at them. "We need to talk about a couple of things. First I want to explain to you why I had gotten so bent out of shape before. I have a past too and I want to share some of it with you."

Jenna sat back on the couch and looked seriously at him. "I'm ready to listen."

Keith held her hand and looked like he was deep in thought. "Well, when I was still in Iowa I had met a girl, Christy. She became my girlfriend, and along with my best friend Tom, we became the perfect trio. The three of us went out together all the time and I felt blessed. I never had to choose between my best friend and my girlfriend, since they got along so well. I was on "cloud nine," as some people would have described it. Well, Tom and Christy would laugh and give each other hugs when we went our separate ways. They were close, but I never knew how close. I'd seen them glance at each other or hug just a little too long, but I didn't think anything of it. Why would I? I could trust them right? Anyways, I would just smile and felt like the luckiest guy in the world to have them both in his life. In the end I trusted them both, and never imagined they would ever betray me. Then finally, after a year of good times I felt it was time to ask Christy to marry me. I had shopped for days to find the perfect ring, and when I did, I rushed to Tom's place to tell him, and ask him to be my best man. I felt like I had found the perfect bride and wanted my best friend to help me come up with the most memorable proposal. I wanted to surprise Christy, but I was the one who got the surprise. Keith took a drink from his glass and took a deep breath. He continued. "When I knocked on the door, I could hear music and knew Tom was home. He opened the door with money in his hand, I assumed, to pay for some food. But when I saw his expression, I knew something was not right. I pushed past him without a word, and walked into the living room. There on the couch, Christy was sitting in a negligee with more skin showing then was covered up. She was sitting provocatively and I could do nothing but stare." Keith paused. "I felt like I was in a bad dream. Then I looked into her eyes I saw a look of surprise that turned quickly to shame. I didn't know what to do. I fell to my knees in front of her, and looked at her in disbelief. I could feel the ring in my pocket and it felt like it was burning a hole into my skin. It felt like forever before I stood up and took a step back. I tried to speak, but my mouth was dry as a desert. I knew I had to get out or something bad would happen. I was mad. I looked at Christy, one last time, and turned to leave. I never wanted to see her again. Then when I got to Tom, who was still standing by the door, I wanted to spit in his face, but decided against it and walked out. As I walked away I heard pleading voices, but I was not going to stay and listen. I didn't know how to feel or how to proceed with what I had just discovered. I'd never been so hurt before and didn't know what to do." Keith looked down and rubbed his legs with his hands. "So, needless to say, the next days and weeks and months were hard to handle. I tried to keep my mind on work. Then when I saw a listing for a transfer, I pounced on it. I needed and wanted a fresh start to get back on my own two feet. I packed my things and headed east" Keith took Jenna's hands in his and stared into her eyes. "So what I'm saying is, even though I did not get hurt physically, I still got hurt. I had two of the people I thought I could trust use my trust against me. I have trouble with having faith in others too. I want you to know that I'm willing to trust in you if you are willing to do the same with me."

Jenna gave Keith a hug and kissed his cheek. "That had to take a lot for you to tell me that story. I'm sorry that it happened to you. I know that it won't be easy all the time, but I'm willing to try and trust. Of course, I can't guarantee that I'll be able to trust one hundred percent in a day or week or months. What happened to me goes down really deep in my subconscious mind. It's going to take a while to work it out. If you're willing to be patient with me I promise that I'm not going to hurt you the way she did. I learned from my trip to Pennsylvania that you are my one and only and I have to have you in my life. In a good way, that is."

Keith touched Jenna's cheek. "That sounds good." He frowned before spoke again. "Now, onto the next subject. We need to talk about Neil. I know you don't want to but it's a topic that has to be discussed."

Jenna gasped. "No. I don't want to talk about him. It's been wonderful today. Don't ruin it. Please."

He looked at her with sympathetic eyes. "I'm sorry but we need to talk about him. He was at your house and Kathy said he called you. This is something we need to address."

Jenna stared at the actors on the television being cheerful and laughing. She wanted to be them at that moment and shrugged when she knew there was no escape from the conversation. "What do you want to talk about? Kathy said that you approached him and told him to stay away. What more is there to talk about?"

"I know what I did and said to him. But I don't know if it was enough. I don't want you to get hurt by him later because we let our guards down." He lowered his head. "I heard what he said. He definitely has a problem with you and he did not have very nice things to say."

Jenna exhaled. "What did you expect? Him to say nice things? I could've told you he would've put me down. He always demoralized me. He's a bad man and has a black heart." Jenna looked at Keith and tried to smile. "Well, it's been a few days since you took care of him, right? He probably went home. Why would he stay here when he knows you'll be around?"

"Jenna, it's just … He didn't seem like he was going to leave til he got what he wanted." Keith seemed frustrated that Jenna wasn't taking this as serious as he wanted her to. "He drove from Idaho, for crying out loud. He didn't just come here for a visit. He came for a reason and I don't want to find out what that reason is. I'm worried."

Jenna took Keith's hands and held them tight. She looked at him and tried to show she was not scared. "Hey, I tell you what. Since I met you I feel like I've become stronger. You're my hero." She smiled and squeezed his hands in hers. "I really do think that he went home but if he calls or comes to my house, I will not be the victim. I promise." She crossed her heart with her fingers. "I know you are worried and I have to admit, I'm a little too, but I can't live my life anymore being afraid of what *might* happen. I need to live in the moment and enjoy what I can." She put her hand on his face and felt the stubble growing. "He can't hurt me anymore. He has no control over me and if the time comes, I'll let him know that too."

Keith stared at her. "Okay. If you think he has left then I'll drop it. I just … " He let out a breath. "I just found you and I don't want to lose you. Please just be careful. You can stay here tomorrow when I go to work. I don't want you going to your house without me just yet." He paused. "At least let me follow you to the house tomorrow and check to make sure it's safe. If not for you, then for me. I want to make sure you are okay by yourself."

Jenna smiled and appreciated his sentiment. "I promise I'll be careful but I have to go home. I can't hide out the rest of my life. Are you going to take me home every day? You can't check for the boogie man before I go to bed at night. That's not going to happen." She paused. "I did that job in Pennsylvania and they are expecting the results soon and you don't have any of the tools I need." She looked around the room. "Well, at least not that I've seen."

Keith shook his head and wasn't going to argue anymore. He pulled Jenna close to him and held her tight. Jenna cuddled next to him and exhaled, happy to have such a wonderful man in her life.

As the day turned into night Keith took her hand and led her back to the bedroom. They rekindled their earlier fire before falling onto the bed intertwined and exhausted. Jenna felt more secure than she had her entire life. She squeezed Keith's hand and he held her tight against him while she listened to his breathing and it became hypnotic. She fell asleep.

# chapter 25

THE NEXT MORNING Keith headed for work and left Jenna alone. He gave her a kiss and told her to stay as long as she wanted but before he shut the door he gave her a quick worried glance. Jenna knew he was concerned but she was happier than she had been in a long time and was not going to think of anything negative. Before he left, she promised to call him after she got to her house to reassure him it was okay.

She stretched as he closed the door and had an urge to lie around all day and wait for him. But she had work to do too. She lingered in bed for a while longer but soon Shadow needed out and they both needed some breakfast.

Jenna dressed in the clothes she wore the day before, wrote Keith a note, and then she and Shadow left. They went down the stairs and out into the sunshine of the day. Jenna was in a terrific mood and couldn't wait for Keith to be done with work. They planned on going to dinner and then for him to experience a night at her house next.

She had not been to her house since she left for Pennsylvania and knew there was some housework waiting for her. The flowers and lawn would need watering. Some dusting would have to be done along with her laundry. But before she started any of that, she needed to start the tedious job of cropping and adjusting the pictures from the battle. She decided to download the pictures and while she waited she would at least water the flowers. She was sure they would be thirsty from her being gone.

When she and Shadow got to the house, Jenna saw the garbage can that contained the flowers Neil had sent. When she peered into it she saw the flowers were shriveled and brown. She shook her head, pushed the can to the side, and opened the front door. When they entered the house Jenna got an uncomfortable feeling, but when Shadow didn't seem to notice anything in the house, it put her mind at ease.

She called Keith and walked around the house as she spoke to him, glancing behind doors and under beds. He sounded worried but as she checked around she reassured him there was nothing there and that Shadow would let her know if there was. She told him she would keep the doors locked and see him tonight for dinner.

After hanging up she threw her new quilt on her bed then took a long shower deciding to let her hair air dry. After she got dressed she went and made some coffee with a couple of slices of toast with butter and cinnamon. Shadow was already eating his breakfast and Jenna went to the computer to download the photos while she ate her toast and drank her coffee. Since she knew the computer would be working a while to download the hundreds of pictures she had taken, she walked into the backyard to water her flowers.

As she stepped into the backyard she got an uneasy feeling again but figured it was from the drama that happened before she left. She shook her head and chuckled to herself before positioning the new birdhouse next to her flower garden and grabbed a water hose.

The flowers scent wafted to her from the coolness of the water she sprayed them with, and they smelled wonderful. Jenna breathed in the aromas and beamed. She couldn't believe that her life had finally turned into something wonderful and she couldn't believe her luck had finally come back to her. She felt like she could lift her feet off the ground and float.

After relishing in the backyard and beautiful weather, Jenna groaned and felt jealous as she left Shadow out to enjoy the sunshine. Dragging her feet, she went inside and sat in front of her computer. She rolled her shoulders and knew they would be aching by the end of the day and thought maybe she could get Keith to rub them for her later. She got goose bumps just thinking of his hands touching her skin and couldn't wait to have him next to her.

Just as the last of the photos downloaded onto her computer, she heard Shadow barking in the yard. She rolled her eyes and wondered what cat he had chased up a tree this time. It always took so much coaxing to get him far enough away so the cat could jump down and run off. She sighed and headed to the door to save the animal he had trapped and by time she got to the door he was scratching frantically to get inside. Jenna found herself almost running to let him in. "I'm coming. I'm coming."

She opened the door for Shadow and he ran past her with a yelp. Jenna was startled by his behavior and watched him as he ran down the hall to the bedroom. She shrugged, figuring a cat had finally fought back and scratched his nose. She giggled to herself and turned to close the door. The door got pushed back at her.

The door's edge hit her on the forehead and she lost her footing as she stepped back. She fell onto her side and when she looked towards the backyard she saw boots at the bottom of the doorway. Instantly, she was overcome with fear as she followed the boots up to the jeans, to the shirt, to the face. She tried to scoot backwards and stand at the same time. The throbbing in her ears from hitting her head was deafening and she tried to grasp the counter to stand up.

Jenna didn't get further than the doorway from the kitchen before a hand gripped her arm with painful force. She tried to pull it away but the grip was too strong. Feeling trapped she started to kick and scream, desperate to get away, but she was pushed back to the floor. Her heart was racing and she could feel blood sliding down the top of her nose. She blinked past the pain and looked up, afraid for her life.

"Hello, Jenna. Happy to see me?" Neil asked calmly.

Jenna put her hand to her head, looked at it, and saw the blood. She glared up at him. "What do you want?"

He pointed at her while holding a half empty whiskey bottle. "We have some unfinished business to tend to. You see, you did not treat me good. After all I did for you," he said in a contemptuous voice.

Jenna did not know what to do. She pulled her knees to the front of her chest and wrapped her arms around her legs. Even from the floor she could smell the whiskey on his breath and knew that hard liquor made him mean. While she tried to think of an escape she slowly looked around the kitchen for any kind of weapon.

Neil seemed to know what she was thinking. He shook his finger at her like she was a little kid doing something wrong. "Tisk-tisk. Now don't be getting any ideas of grabbing a knife or nothing. I'll kill you if you try." He leaned against the counter and crossed his legs. His boots clicked when they hit against each other and he talked in an eerie calm tone. "I just wanted to come and talk a bit. When I saw you last it ended on such a bad note. You looked pretty out there watering the flowers, by the way. It looks like you finally lost those last few pounds of fat. Don't know why you didn't do that when you were with me. But you seem so peaceful and happy. Well, I want that too, Jenna." His voice got louder. "I want to be happy but you put me in jail because I accidently pushed you a little hard. How am I supposed to be happy when my friends look at me like I'm a wife beater?" he stood up straight and rolled his shoulders and turned his neck until it made a cracking sound. His tone became harsh and demeaning. "Jenna, tell me, how am I supposed to be happy? Huh? How, Jenna?"

The hairs stood up on the back of Jenna's arms and neck. He had so much hate in his voice. He seemed different then when she had known him in the past. He acted even colder and had a darker side than she had ever known him to have. She needed to think, and quickly. She spoke softly. "I'm sorry, Neil. You have always been stronger than me. I'd be a fool to try anything to hurt you. But I don't know how to answer you. I didn't know how to make you happy when I was with you. I tried everything I could to keep you satisfied to make us both happy. For crying out loud, I gave up my family for you." Jenna felt heat growing in her stomach and knew this would be her only chance to find out the truth. She spoke calmly and quietly. "I have a few questions for you, if that's alright. Why was it all right for you to cheat on me with other women but I could not even have a friend to talk to? Why did you stay who you were but I had to change everything? Why did you treat me like a piece of property when I gave my heart to you? Why couldn't you love me the way I had tried love you?" Jenna watched for a reaction and Neil's demeanor changed. He got a blank look on his face and looked like he was a thousand miles away. He stood detached for a few moments before he blinked, took a drink from the whiskey bottle, and looked at her with hate.

"Why did I do all of those things? Because you were weak! Why would you let me take you away from your family? Why would I not take advantage of such a weak woman and mold her into the perfect little wife. I thought it was fun, okay. I thought it was fun to watch you bend and twist and do anything I wanted you to. I thought it was funny to watch you beg to get attention. I laughed about it when I went out with my buddies and knew you would be at home waiting for me." He paused before speaking in a deep and quiet voice. "I have to say that when I first met you that I wanted something more from you but you never gave it to me. I wanted to love you. I had tried, in the beginning, but then it started to be a game … for me. I would give myself a deadline for a new goal. How long it would take for you to cut your hair. How long it would take for you to give up everything for me." Neil stretched and arched his back. "I have to say that you were ahead of schedule on quite a few things." Neil chuckled to himself then took a big, long drink from the whiskey bottle and looked hard at Jenna. "You were a toy and nothing else."

Jenna could not believe what she heard. How could a man be so cold and treat another human being this way? How was it that she was the one that got trapped in the web with him? She knew he was trying to demoralize her to nothing and she wasn't going to let it happen. She needed to get away from him. She slowly moved and tried to get up. "I'm sorry for … "

Neil kicked towards her striking the air beside her face. "Oh, shut up! I don't want to hear your babbling anymore!" He kicked again and this time he hit her in the arm with the toe of his boot. She felt a pain radiate through her left arm. When she leaned forward from the pain, he kicked again. His boot hit her on the side of the head and then her face. She heard a loud ringing and then everything went blurry.

Jenna fell to the floor. She heard Neil laughing and the sloshing of the whiskey bottle as he took a drink then everything went completely dark.

# Chapter 26

MOANING, SHE began to stir. Pain shot through her head and arm. She wiped blood from her mouth and saw dry blood on the floor under where her head had been. As she waited for some of the pain to subside she had no idea how long she had been lying there. Trying to listen through the ringing in her ears, she couldn't tell if she was alone or not. She tried to sit up but felt like she would get sick if she moved her head off the floor too quickly. Attempting to move quietly, she almost screamed as she moved her left arm and had to bite her lip to be quiet. She knew her arm was broken.

She tried to listen hard and could not hear anything. She could not hear any cars going by or birds singing. She could not even hear Shadow.

After a few minutes she slowly tried to sit up without getting queasy or applying pressure to her arm. As she raised her head off the floor it felt like it was going to explode from the pressure behind her eyes. She didn't know if she had a concussion and needed a doctor but she wished one would come through the door at that moment.

It took a great amount of energy to get up to her knees. She had to move so slowly and the pain going through her body was intense. But she needed to get to a phone and that is what she concentrated on. Her vision was slightly blurred and she couldn't see into the other rooms. She was petrified when she heard a movement coming from the living room. She whispered, "Shadow?"

"You didn't think I would leave so soon, did you?" Neil asked, slurring his words.

Jenna almost fell back onto the floor when she heard his voice. He sounded even more intoxicated which made him even more dangerous. But also slower.

Jenna pushed through the pain and nausea and stood up. She leaned on the counter for support but couldn't raise her head completely from the throbbing pain. The song she had heard the day before, about becoming a stronger woman, played in her head and she was not going to let him win, at least not without a fight. She felt groggy and had to focus as Neil stood up from the couch and came into the kitchen.

He staggered towards her. "You think you have got tougher through the years? Obviously not by the way you couldn't even handle a little kick to the head. You're lucky I didn't have my way with you while you were passed out. I could've, you know." He raised his bottle into the air. "But I wanted to see your eyes. We are far from done here."

Jenna swayed as she tried to stay alert and to keep standing on her feet. She could see the whiskey bottle in his hand and when she squinted at it, she could tell it was almost empty. For a moment she was glad he was drinking so much and he would not be able to perform. The thought of him touching her made her shudder.

She looked towards the counter. The digits on the microwave clock were blurry. She strained to make out the shape of the numbers and she could see it was almost five thirty. She tried to comprehend that she had laid on the floor for hours and Neil sat and watched her lay in her own blood. What kind of man was he? She was thankful she wasn't dead.

Neil came closer and he had to lean on the wall to stay standing. She could smell his breath was saturated with whiskey and his eyes were bloodshot. One eye was black and blue and she wondered if that was Keith's handy work. She couldn't help but smirk as she thought about Keith punching him.

"What's so funny? You think this is funny?" Neil asked as he staggered again and almost fell.

Jenna felt it was her only chance to get away. She needed to be able to move without him reacting quickly. She took a breath and looked at him. "Actually, yes, I think it's funny. It's hilarious," she said as she held her throbbing head in her right hand.

"Oh, really. Maybe I need to teach you another lesson," Neil said with his face red and angry.

Jenna's eyes darted around the room for something to use to defend herself and took a small step closer to the sink. She had to work hard to stay focused and push away the pain radiating through her body. Every word she said sent blasts of pain through her head. She had to speak softly and quietly. "You can't do anything to me. You're a drunk, ugly, weak man. I can't believe that I stayed with you. I guess I felt sorry for you and didn't want you to be alone." She saw his expression get even angrier and almost distorted. He held on to the wall as he tried to move closer to her. Jenna took another step towards the sink and kept talking to distract him. "Maybe I was playing a game with you. Did you ever think of that? Maybe I was taking pictures of you when you were drunk and passed out next to the toilet or on the floor half naked. Maybe I kept them to put on the internet to have a good laugh about it. Maybe I had someone come to the house when you went to bar and was happy with him when you were gone." She knew her voice was soft and didn't know how much he actually heard. But she knew her last comment had been listened to and had pushed him over the edge. She knew he didn't like the thought of losing control over his prey.

"You … You … " Neil took a large step and grabbed for the counter so he wouldn't fall to the floor. Jenna moved to the side and he fell against the counter. She went to step across the room and he got a hold of her hair. She screamed from the pain in her already aching head. Jenna kicked at his knee-cap and connected with it hard. He let go of her hair and hit his head, on the counter, as he bent down. He dropped the whiskey bottle and grabbed his head with his hands.

Jenna couldn't help but laugh at him. "How does it feel?"

She suddenly felt a new energy and was not going to be the victim. No more feeling abused. No longer would she be scared.

Neil stood up and glared at her. He had slobber in the corners of his mouth when he spoke. "I will show you pain!"

Just as Neil ended his sentence Shadow came into the room. Jenna didn't know where he had been but she was happy to see he was all right.

Shadow started to bark and growl at Neil. He charged at Neil and then backed away just as fast.

Neil was distracted by the barking and turned his attention toward Shadow momentarily. He tried to kick at Shadow, holding on to the counter for support, and missed each time. He cursed at Shadow and tried over and over to kick him with his boot.

Jenna saw that this was her chance and turned to the sink. Above it hung a cast iron skillet, with an ocean mural painted on the bottom.

She took a big step and reached for it. The hook it was hanging from tore from the wall, leaving a hole. Neil turned towards her and reached for her arm. Jenna held the skillet with both hands and screamed as she swung it like a bat. It connected with Neil's head and he fell to the floor. She screamed again from the pain in her arm and dropped the skillet.

Shadow had his tail between his legs and was shaking. Jenna looked at him and tried to control the tremors of her hands. "It's okay, boy, we got him. Good boy! I didn't know you had a tough side to you." She leaned back against the sink holding back the urge to vomit. She waited for the pain to subside and watched Neil to see if he would move.

On the floor was a pool of blood from the blow to his head. She did not know if he was dead but was satisfied he did not get back up.

Keeping an eye on him, Jenna backed away and went to get a phone. Through the throbbing pain in her head she could not think where she had left her cell phone so she turned to the landline. Forgetting that she had unplugged it before she went to Pennsylvania, she was going to have to plug the landline into the wall before she could dial. Her hands shook uncontrollably and it took multiple attempts before she got a ring tone. Holding the phone in her hand, she dialed 911. She could not remember what she said but minutes later she heard sirens in the distance.

# chapter 27

JENNA FELT LIKE she was in and out of consciousness as she saw a police officer come through the front door. She didn't know how he got in, she was sure it had been locked, but she couldn't remember for sure. He showed her a badge and she could make out a shape of a gun by his side before he put an arm around her and led her to the couch. She could feel the couch cushion sink down as he sat beside her, but everything became blurry and she wasn't for sure who was actually there.

Fear penetrated her mind with the thought that it could be Neil. What if he had hit the officer on the head with his whiskey bottle and he was the one sitting next to her? With that thought, she tried to stand and escape but then felt a hand pull her gently back down to the couch. She heard a pleading voice asking her to stay seated. A soothing voice. A voice with no anger bubbling from his words.

Trying to focus, she turned her head to the side and squinted to concentrate on the man's face. She could make out a few facial features and could tell it was an older man with a bald head. She felt herself relax and her eyes grew heavy.

Trying to stay awake she could see that the officer looked like he was afraid to touch her. She wondered how bad her injuries were and wanted to cry but didn't even have the strength to do that.

The man's voice seemed to be so far away, but she could hear him ask if she was all right. Jenna didn't know if she had responded.

Then in the distance, behind the high pitched ringing in her ears, she could make out the sound of Shadow barking. This was followed by soothing muffles of words, as she assumed the officer tried to coax Shadow to calm down. But then, just as fast, she saw a blur of white as Shadow ran down the hall, towards the bedroom. Jenna wanted to yell for him, to come to her, but couldn't make her mouth say the words.

She closed her eyes and when she opened them again, she saw a stretcher removing Neil from the house and a paramedic was kneeled down in front of her. He was trying to remove some of the blood from her nose to see how bad the injury was. She looked past him and tried to watch as Neil was carried out the door but couldn't hold her head up long enough. So instead, she tried to focus on the paramedic in front of her but could not see him very clearly either. He seemed to be two or three men weaving side to side. They would go behind each other to make it look like one man for a moment and then would weave again to look like three.

Jenna heard the paramedic asking questions as the officer had. Again, she did not know if her lips even moved to give him an answer. She could only feel pain radiating throughout her face and didn't know if she could talk if she wanted to. She only wanted to sleep and no one would let her. Every time she would close her eyes there would be someone shaking her good arm or snapping their fingers in front of her face. Why wouldn't they let her sleep?

It felt like she had been sitting on the couch for hours upon hours which had turned into days before she heard a man hollering outside. She could hear him hollering her name over and over. The sound got louder as he got closer to the house. He finally quit yelling when he came through the front door.

Jenna looked up to see Keith, as he entered her house, and he instantly took a step back towards the door when he saw her. She saw him gasp and couldn't imagine what he saw. Keith fell to his knees in front of her and stared. When he spoke it sounded like he was going to burst into tears. "I ... Why did this happen? Why wasn't I here for you? How did you ... You need to go to the hospital." Keith looked over at the officer that was sitting next to Jenna on the couch.

The officer looked back with sympathetic eyes. "Yes sir, she is going now. We just arrived on the scene a few minutes ago." The officer got up from the couch and yelled a command, to a paramedic, for her to get to the hospital immediately.

Keith got up from his knees and sat down next to Jenna. He reached out to touch her arm and she moaned from the pain. Jenna turned her head slowly and looked at him with bloodshot eyes. Her voice sounded raspy and soft. "I won." She tried to smile but couldn't from the pain in around her mouth.

As she spoke paramedics came into the house to take her to the hospital. They brought in a stretcher but she refused. Even through all the pain, she knew she wanted to finish this on her own two feet.

Jenna could see the worry in Keith's eyes as she tried to get up from the couch and walk. She wanted to hug Keith but she was too tired. She was too weak to even try and knew it was going to take help to get her to the ambulance.

As she limped outside, she tried to focus her eyes. She could see the stretcher with Neil lying on it. He was still unconscious. He had handcuffs attaching his wrists to the metal side rail which meant he was still alive. She couldn't believe that she had overcome him and that he now lying lifeless in front of her.

Jenna began to shake and got weaker when she thought about what had just happened. She was glad for the support of the paramedic beside her or she would have fallen to the ground.

The walk to the ambulance seemed to take forever and she wanted to lie down and take a long nap. She wanted to wake up from a bad dream and wake to the day of her and Keith at the beach with the ponies. She wanted to start over and make everything less complicated. But the pounding in her head reminded her that this was real and she was going to have to deal with it.

She looked around for Keith and felt an aching go through her arm as she tried to turn. She saw him walk quickly towards her and as he got closer she could see the worry grow in his expression. Jenna spoke but did not know how clear her words were. "I need you to do something."

Keith tried to smile. "Anything. Just name it."

Jenna tried to forget the throbbing in her head as she spoke but then started to feel dizzy. She held her head with her right hand and tried to steady her feet. "Shadow. Is he okay?" She was whispering as she finished her sentence.

Keith rubbed his temples. "I don't know. I can check but I wanted to follow you to the hospital. You are more of my concern right now. But I'll check for you." He looked towards the paramedic. "Which hospital are you taking her too?"

Jenna cut in before the paramedic could speak. Her voice was quiet, almost inaudible. Both men had to lean towards her to hear her words. "Call John and Kathy. My parents. The numbers are in a drawer ... in a drawer.

Please." Jenna got dizzier and started to sway. The paramedic said something to her but she could not understand his words. Her legs became weak and everything became blurry. Her legs didn't want to hold her up anymore and she felt herself falling. She heard Keith yelling her name over and over. His voice seemed to sound further and further away until she could not hear him at all. Everything turned dark and she became unconscious.

# chapter 28

THE STORM DROVE rain against the house windows and Jenna almost felt like they were going to crack from the force. She sat on the couch and hugged Shadow while he whimpered in her arms. The darkness momentarily lit up from lightning crashing through and it made the night seem eerie and unreal.

A loud rumble of thunder shook the house and Jenna jumped when she heard someone banging on the door. Reluctantly she let go of Shadow and proceeded to open it. There was a man, wearing a hat with rain dripping from the brim. He was looking at the ground and when he raised his head Jenna was struck with fear. She backed up from the door and fell onto a chair. Shadow started to bark and growl as the man entered the house.

The man walked towards Jenna and raised his hand to strike her. Jenna raised her arms in defense and waited for the blow of his wrath. Just then lightning struck the ground in front of the house and lit the room like the sun. The man screamed from the brightness and shriveled into a heap of dust on the floor.

Jenna fluttered her eyes open and saw nothing but white. Blinking her eyes to see clearly, she saw she was in the hospital and it had been a dream. Another bad dream.

Her head was pounding and when she moved, her body it felt like she had been run over by a car. She felt something warm against her hand and she followed her arm down to see it was Keith's hand holding hers. Then when she looked at her wrist she saw a tube attached which she assumed was for the pain and was happy to have it. Her vision was not as blurry and some of the pain had subsided, but not enough.

Carefully, she followed his hand up to his arm and then to his face. His expression was a mixture of admiration and empathy. She tilted her head to the side and tried to smile. Her voice was hoarse and weak. "Hey there, stranger. I feel like someone took a hammer to my face. How bad do I look?"

Keith leaned closer and gently kissed the top of her hand. He rubbed her arm and stared at her with love. "Hey sunshine, you look … "

"That says it all. Don't say anymore." She didn't know if she wanted him to look at her but it was obviously too late. She watched as Keith's expression turned to remorse.

"Jenna I should have been there. I told you I would be there for you. I wasn't. I should have made sure he left town before you came home." Keith put his head in his hands and tried to control his emotions. "I can't imagine what you felt. I should've been there."

Jenna tried to keep her sentences short to keep her mouth from hurting. "It wasn't your fault. You warned me. I'm bullheaded and stubborn. I'm okay. Really, I am. My wounds will heal. I'm sure I look like a monster but it will go away."

"But I should have … "

Jenna interrupted. "No. Don't say any more. It's not your fault."

Keith's voice got louder and more demanding. "Now listen. I'm the man. I should've taken care of this for you. You shouldn't be in a hospital bed because of … because of that man." He stood up and tried to pace to get some of the adrenaline out of him. "Bottom line I should have … " Keith looked over at Jenna and saw her trying to smile at him. "What?"

"Keith, I beat him. I won. I took care of it and won." She felt tears stream down her face.

He sat back down and held her hand. "You're right. You didn't need me. You kicked ass and took him down!" Keith smiled. "I'm the proudest man in the world. You're beautiful, talented, and can kick ass too. I guess I better watch out if I ever make you mad."

Jenna started to laugh but stopped just as fast when she felt the pain from her lip and head. She held her head with her hand and tried to stop the pain.

"I'm sorry. I didn't mean to make you hurt." Keith rubbed her right arm.

Just then John and Kathy came bursting in the door. Kathy looked frantic and John looked scared. When they looked at Jenna both of their expressions became horrified sympathy.

Kathy was the first to get close to Jenna and studied her face. "Well, what did you do to him?" she asked.

Jenna saw Kathy's expression and frowned. She concentrated on not moving her mouth as much as possible when she spoke. "Hey I'm all right. Everything will heal. I took care of him with the cast iron skillet I got from that shop next to your diner." She smiled then grimaced.

Kathy laughed and relaxed. "A cast iron skillet huh? That's one for the books. Good job girl."

John stood in the background and couldn't bring himself to get any closer to Jenna. He looked at the floor and shook his head like a guilty father looking at a daughter he did not help.

Jenna watched as Keith walked over to John. He put his hand on John's shoulder and spoke with pride. "Can you believe Jenna handled herself so well and kicked that guy's butt? She is the winner of all winners."

John looked at Keith and knew what he was doing. He beamed. "You're right." John walked over to Jenna and kissed her gently on top of her head. "Good job sweetie. I'm a proud ... " he stopped.

"Dad?" Jenna finished for him and attempted to smile. "I'm proud to be your daughter too."

John looked away for a moment to swallow back tears and wiped his nose with a handkerchief. When he looked back at her, Jenna knew he acknowledged that in some way, she was his daughter. Not by blood, but still his daughter. She knew John was proud of her. "John, I'm happy to see that you are better. I was scared when I first saw you in the hospital too."

John nodded. "Yeah, but when I was in hospital, I was sleeping and did not see the worry in your eyes. It breaks my heart to see you like this and I hope *that man* gets everything he deserves. It makes me sick when a man takes advantage of a woman. Us men are supposed to protect you and he did you so wrong. But you took care of the situation and I'm so proud of you for handling yourself."

Jenna's lip began to bleed when she tried to smile. She dabbed at it with a tissue and tried not to show the pain. Even though the medicine helped a little her head was still throbbing and her arm ached. The ice on her arm seemed to make the pain worse and she wanted her mom. She looked at Keith. "Did you call my family? I need them to know what happened and that I'm okay."

Keith shrugged his shoulders. "Actually, no. I didn't know if you had told them about me or anything. I felt really out of place to talk to your parents' and them not be comfortable with a stranger telling them. So I thought if it's okay, that Kathy would call them. I'm sure that they know about her, right? "

Jenna spoke softly and her eyes got heavy. "I understand. I didn't tell them anything about us. I guess I'm scared how they'll react." Jenna looked at Kathy. "Would you please call my family?"

Kathy rubbed Jenna's leg. "Of course I would honey. I'd be glad to," Kathy said and smiled.

After a visiting a few more minutes Jenna could not keep her eyes open any longer. She wanted to sleep to forget the pain for a while. She told everyone she was going to fall asleep and John and Kathy gave her a kiss and left the room to let her rest. Keith remained behind and held her hand as she closed her eyes.

When she opened her eyes again, it was dark. She looked to the side and saw Keith slouched in a chair asleep. He looked peaceful and Jenna watched as his chest rose and fell with his breaths. She felt safe with him beside her and couldn't remember when she had felt completely safe before. She imagined it was when her dad had held her when she had fallen off her bike or when her mom cuddled with her when she had been sick. Jenna ached to have her parents with her and wondered if they were called to let them know she was all right. She didn't care if they told them what happened, she just wanted them to know she was safe.

"You're awake." A nurse said and sounded surprised as she entered the room. "I didn't think we would see you awake until the morning or even the afternoon."

Jenna wrinkled her brow. Her voice was still rough and soft. "What time is it? How long have I been asleep?"

"It's about three in the morning. You have been asleep for quite a while. But that is to be expected. I was just checking your fluids from your IV. Do you want anything while I'm here? How is the pain level?"

"The pain is a lot less. Could I get some apple juice?"

"Not a problem." The nurse said and looked towards Keith. "Looks like someone else is up too. Sorry if I woke you."

Keith watched the nurse leave the room and directed his attention to Jenna. "Hey there. How are you feeling?"

"I suppose I feel as good as I look. I feel like a truck hit me. But it doesn't hurt to talk as much. The medicine must be working better."

Keith moved his chair closer to the bed and held Jenna's hand. He stared into her eyes. "I was really afraid. When I went to your house and saw the cops. At first I thought it was a neighbor, or maybe I just wanted it to be. But I never thought I would see something like that to someone I care for. You don't know how bad I wanted to take Neil off that stretcher and hurt him even more."

"I'm sure you did. But it wouldn't have done any good."

"Yes it would have. It would have given me some satisfaction."

"Well, I took care of him pretty good. Have you heard anyone say how he is? Did I … kill him?" Jenna didn't know how to feel when she asked that. She felt emotions of remorse but she also felt emotions of pleasure if he was dead.

"All I heard was that he was taken here and then when they found out the circumstances they moved him to a different hospital. I know he is not dead though. I'm just glad he's gone. I didn't like the idea of him being in the same hospital. It would make me very uncomfortable so I could imagine it would you too."

"Yeah. I don't want him anywhere near me. Ever."

The nurse walked in with some apple juice with a straw and left just as fast. Jenna took a drink and enjoyed the coolness on her throat. She took a couple more sips and looked at Keith. "Did you find Shadow? He was awesome you know. He charged at Neil and let me have time to get the skillet."

Keith frowned. "Well, I did find him but he is not acting like himself. He was hiding behind a basket in your room and would not even come to me. I sat on the floor and talked to him for a while and he finally sat down a few feet from me but wouldn't get any closer. He was cowered down and I think he is confused. I think he really misses you."

Jenna tried not to cry. She was tired of crying. "Is he all right then? Where is he? He wasn't hurt was he?"

Jenna thought back and knew that Neil had been trying to kick Shadow. She did not know if Neil had kicked him the way she had been or if he had been hurt at all. Her heart began to pound hard and she couldn't bear the thought of Shadow being hurt because of her.

Keith patted Jenna's leg with his hand. "He's fine. He wasn't limping and I didn't see any blood or anything on him. It would have been pretty easy to see with his white fur. I filled his bowl with food and gave him some fresh water. I didn't know what else to do. I had to get here with you."

Jenna wanted Keith to go back to the house. She wanted him to take care of Shadow. But then she looked into his worried eyes and knew it was going to have to wait. She could not ask him to do something like that right now. That would not be fair. Besides that it was three in the morning. Shadow would be more afraid with someone coming into the house at this hour. So she tried to picture Shadow lying on her bed sleeping peacefully. "Okay, but can you please go over there tomorrow. Well, I guess later today."

Keith grinned at her and winked. "Yes Jenna, I'll do that first thing *after* I talk to the doctor and he says you're fine."

Jenna felt butterflies in her stomach when Keith winked at her. She was in love with him, there was no denying it. "Hey, I wanted to say sorry for not telling my parents about you. I really am not ashamed of you. If anything you are the best thing to ever happen to me. I do love you Keith Christensen."

"I know you do and I won't ever take it for granted."

# chapter 29

JENNA SMELLED WARM toast and scrambled eggs. She opened her eyes and saw a tray in front of her and wondered how long she had been asleep this time. She glanced around the room and was alone.

She didn't like the feeling of being alone and hoped someone would come visit her soon. She didn't want to get lost in her thoughts because she knew where they would lead and she didn't want to relive her night with Neil.

Concentrating on the food in front of her, she took a bite and couldn't remember the last time she had eaten. She devoured the food and did not stop until there was not a morsel left on her plate. Just as she wiped her mouth with a napkin Kathy and John entered the room. Jenna smiled. "Hey there. I'm so happy to see you both."

Kathy gave Jenna a kiss on her head. "You're looking so much better. I can't believe what a difference a day makes."

"Well, that's a good thing to hear. I hope I don't look as bad as I feel though. I can talk easier now without my mouth and head hurting." Jenna looked towards the door. "Did you happen to see a nurse? I'm still hungry?" Jenna paused and looked around the room. "Where's Keith? In the bathroom?"

John sat on the bed beside Jenna and exhaled. "We saw him on the way in here. He said something about Shadow and making sure he was all right. What's wrong with Shadow?"

Jenna wrinkled her forehead and then remembered they had no idea what happened. No one did. She hadn't told them. "Shadow was the reason I escaped Neil. He came into the room, charged Neil, and gave me time to think. I don't know if I would look this good if he hadn't been there." Jenna paused and thought about what might have happened. "I might not be here at all."

John stood up from the bed and stared at Jenna. "It came down to Shadow if you survived or not? That dog is getting a big, juicy steak the next time I see him."

Kathy stood beside John and grabbed his arm. "No, Shadow is going to get anything a dog could possibly want. He is going to be the most spoiled dog ever."

Just then, Jenna heard a familiar voice. She looked towards the door and saw her parents and brother and sister walk through. Jenna couldn't help to not cry and felt such love for them. "Mom. Dad. Julie. Luke. Hi, I ... " she stopped mid-sentence when she saw the expression on their faces. They looked at her with pity and horror. Jenna felt ugly and wanted to hide.

Jenna's mom slowly walked up to her, studying her face. "My baby. Why did this happen to such a wonderful girl. I'm so sorry baby." She hugged Jenna and kissed her cheek.

Slowly the rest of Jenna's family came and hugged and kissed her and tried not to hurt her or stare.

Jenna felt the tension in the air and was about to hide her head under the blankets when she saw Keith walk through the door. He saw her family and looked like he was ready to turn around and head back out. Jenna motioned for him to come next to her and everyone turned their heads. Jenna took Keith's hand in hers and felt the tension in his grip.

Jenna's voice was soft. "Mom and dad, this is Keith. We have been dating for the last few weeks. I'm sorry for not telling you. I've been so confused. I don't know where I stand with you anymore. I have thought a thousand ways to say sorry but none of them seem to be good enough for what I did." Jenna wiped a tear from her cheek and pushed through the headache she was getting. "I'm sorry we have not been close for so long. I'm sorry it took something like this to bring us back together. I'm sorry."

All at once, her entire family was saying it was okay and they understood. But there was an awkward feeling among them which was interrupted when Kathy and John, who had been standing to the back of the room, moved forward.

Kathy looked around to each face and threw her hands in the air. "Oh my! I finally get to meet the family of sweet Jenna. She is the dearest girl I have ever met and I'm so delighted to meet you all. She has told me so much about all of you." With that she started to give each of them a big hug and kiss on the cheek and broke up the tension of the room and replaced it with smiles and laughs.

Through all the new introductions, Keith glanced over at Jenna and he saw tears flowing down her cheeks. He sat down next to her and wiped a tear away. "What's wrong? Do I need to get a nurse?"

As Keith spoke everyone veered around in their direction. Stares of concern came over all of their faces as they stepped closer.

Jenna looked at each of them and attempted to smile. "This is the best thing to ever happen. I feel like I have everyone I love in one room." She wiped her eyes and frowned. "I'm sorry it happened like this." Jenna suddenly felt like an ugly monster and tried to hide her face with her hand. She couldn't imagine how she looked and when everyone looked at her she could tell it wasn't good.

Jenna's mom, Judy, went to her, moved her hand from her face, and held her hand. "My dear little girl, I forgave you the moment you said the words when you left the house so many years ago. I've never been mad at you and I tried to tell you that so many times. I was afraid that you would be lost forever and we would never hold you in our arms again. I hate that it something so bad has brought us together, but I'm still glad that we are here."

Jenna's dad, Tom, chimed in. "Don't worry about how you look. They are just bumps bruises. They'll go away. I can vouch that you had quite a few of them growing up. I'm not going to make fun of you now when I never did then. I'm sure no one else in this room will either. You went through a horrific ordeal and we are all proud of you. Like your mom said, we have never had hard feelings towards you. My only regret is that I didn't come here to tell you that myself. But we all agreed to give you your space for as long as you needed. We love you Jenna and will always love you. You are our daughter. You will always be our daughter. All of us have missed you terribly. Now, quit trying to hide. No one is thinks you look like a monster or think any less of you. We all understand the circumstances and won't judge how you look because of them." He looked to each face in the room and each person nodded their head in agreement. "See there, no one is going to give you any trouble. We just want you healed up and happy."

Everyone nodded their heads in agreement again and smiled at her.

"All right, since I have everyone in the same room I'll try and tell you what happened. I've told a little of my story to John and Kathy but not enough for you all to understand. I'll have to tell the story to the police later today too." Jenna took a deep breath and began to give them as much detail as she could. She had tears running down her face, along with everyone else in the room.

Over the next few minutes she explained the whole ordeal until she finally took the skillet to Neil's head and knocked him down. Everyone congratulated her for her accomplishment and they were so proud of the woman she had become. They shook their heads in disbelief and questioned if they could do the same thing if they had been in that situation. Her brother and sister beamed at her and couldn't wait until they could spend some quality time together and catch up on everything they had missed.

Jenna couldn't believe the emotions she was feeling. In the last weeks she had gone through so many situations from falling in love, to defeating Neil, to reuniting with her family. She could not believe how everything was finally fitting together and become a life that she was ready to live.

# chapter 30

A COUPLE DAYS later, after getting a cast and being released from the hospital Jenna breathed in the clean scent of her house. She took a deep breath and cautiously walked into the kitchen. When she looked around she did not see any remnants of a fight that had taken place there. She looked back at her family amazed. She knew it had to be difficult, physically and mentally, to clean her dried blood from the floor. "I don't know what to say. I wasn't expecting you to clean up. I ... "

Jenna's mom cut her off. "You don't have to say anything. We're your family and we wanted to help. There was no reason for you to come back and experience the memories of what happened by seeing it. Don't worry about it."

"It doesn't look like anything happened at all." Jenna glanced towards the sink and saw the cast iron skillet hanging on its hook, just as it had before. It was clean but had damage on the outer edge. The ocean mural was now disfigured and Jenna knew she would never forget how it happened. "If there wasn't the dent in the skillet I'd start to think it was a bad dream. Thank you so much." Jenna gave everyone a hug and then she heard Shadow bark. She whirled around to see him running towards her. She fell to her knees and kissed his head. "Thank you Shadow. You're my hero." She scratched behind his ears and stood up to look at her family. They had only come to the house to welcome her home and were going to head back to the airport to return to Idaho. Jenna felt sad to lose them so fast. She wished they could stay for a couple more weeks so they could catch up on the last five years they had lost. But she knew that their relationship was on its way to being repaired. Jenna couldn't wait to have closeness with them again. She shook her head and gave them each a huge hug before they said their goodbyes and headed out the door.

Jenna watched as her family drove away in a rental car and saw Keith walking up the sidewalk towards her. He gave her a quick hug. "I wanted to make sure you had your time with them before I intruded."

"Keith, I'm sure that they would have liked to say goodbye to you too."

"Oh, that's okay. I'm sure that I will see them again. Right? Everything is okay now?"

Jenna put her good arm around Keith and exhaled a happy breath. "Yes, yes it is."

# Epilogue

JENNA LOOKED OUT at her yard and admired the differences of the landscape as the fall weather began to take place of the warm summer heat. She laidback on a lounge chair and felt at peace with herself. She watched as fluffy clouds moved slowly with the breeze across a gorgeous sky. The sun was just beginning to hide behind the trees and began to leave exquisite colors that, she felt, even a painter could not capture with their brush. Bringing her attention back to her yard, she saw her flowers moving gently with the light wind and they seemed to dance with it. Then she saw Shadow as he sat under a tree chewing on a rawhide and seemed to be as content as her.

"What are you thinking about?" Keith asked as he entered the backyard.

"Oh, you know. How wonderful my life has become."

"It's even more wonderful since I'm all moved in."

Jenna looked at him astonished. "There are no more boxes?"

"Nope, not one. Everything is put away where it should be and looks pretty good if I say so myself. But I'm sure you're not going to like some of my college stuff and I know I have a problem with some of the items sitting out in the bathroom. I'm sure we'll figure it all out." Keith winked at her. "As long as I get my way."

Jenna shook her head. "Yeah, I'll make sure you get your way. That's how it goes with you men, isn't it?"

Keith sat down in a chair next to Jenna. "Ha ha, very funny."

Jenna took a drink from her glass and looked at Keith. "No, seriously, I was thinking that I don't have to look over my shoulder anymore. And that is a great feeling. And besides that, I talk to my family at least once a week, if not more, and I feel like we are close again." She touched Keith's arm. "And I have a wonderful man beside me, and now living with me, to enjoy this evening."

"Ah shucks. You're going to make me blush." Keith said as he waved his hand in the air. "But on a serious note, I do have to say that you've changed a lot since we first met. And it's all for the better. You have bloomed like a rose into a beautiful, or I should say, an even more beautiful woman. I'm the lucky one." Keith squeezed her hand softly. "I love you, Jenna."

"I love you too," Jenna whispered.

She had waited for months to hear Keith to say those words. It was just three little short words, but they meant so much when they came from someone that she loved also. She was beginning to wonder if he would ever say them. Even after they decided to move in together, he never slipped or tried to say it. But now they were a couple in love. Jenna squeezed Keith's hand and let the words sink in.

She couldn't hide the smile on her face as she looked down at her glass and twirled the straw in her tea. She closed her eyes and tried to remember the last time she was this happy. There had been times when she thought she was happy, but now, feeling like she did, nothing compared.

Jenna's thoughts were interrupted when she heard a rustling in front of her. She looked up to see that Shadow had left his rawhide and was now burrowed in a flower bush.

Jenna giggled as she watched him camouflage himself among the fragrant flowers and greenery. She saw his tail wag from beneath the foliage and noticed that he had found a beautiful black butterfly. He was trying to follow it through the shrubbery, intrigued by it.

As Jenna admired the butterfly gliding effortlessly away from Shadow, it reminded her of the tattoo she had placed on her back so many years ago. And as she watched it soar into the air, she recognized the butterfly's beauty and strength, and saw a reflection of herself.

Made in the USA
Charleston, SC
09 May 2013